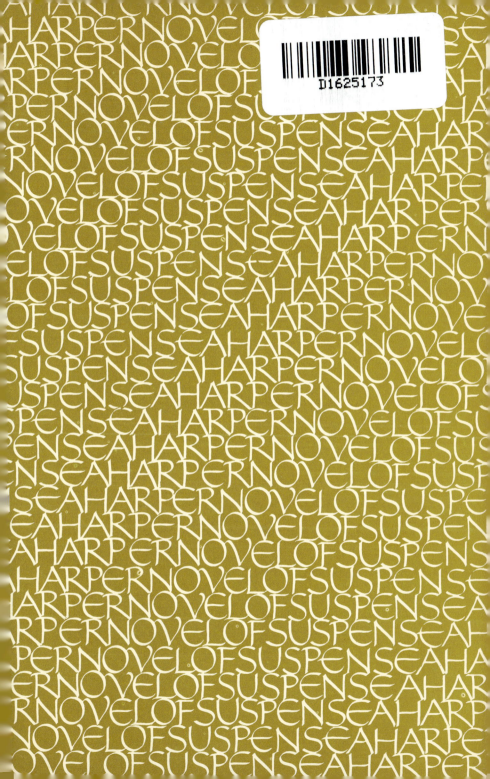

VIRGINIA'S THING

Virginia's Thing

By Henry Woodfin

HARPER & ROW, PUBLISHERS

New York, Evanston, and London

1817

A JOAN KAHN–HARPER NOVEL OF SUSPENSE

FIRST EDITION

LIBRARY OF CONGRESS CATALOG CARD NUMBER: 68-29576

M-S

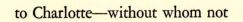

to Charlotte—without whom not

1

IT WAS one of those unseasonably hot May days when the intensity of the heat makes you think you've misread the calendar. When I got off the plane the humidity wrapped itself around me for a greeting; and it didn't loosen its arms as I drove along the throughway to the city.

I was depressed. It had been a lousy job. One of those wandering-broker cases. I'd finally found him in Montreal and he'd become soddenly hysterical, offering to pay me or do anything to let him stay lost. Then it took three days to arrange his shipment back to the glory of the Exchange and the brokerage firm. But I'd felt sorry for the guy and for a while sorry for myself and disgusted with my job. Still, for an ex-cop it provided a living and some independence.

I thought of checking into my office but it was after twelve, I was hot, and my fee for the case was good enough so that I wouldn't have to worry for a couple of months even if nothing else came in. I swung the car toward my apartment and thought of a nap, a shower, and a good dinner.

My watch read one o'clock when I got to the apartment,

and it took a while to glance through a five-day accumulation of mail and to take a shower which did nothing to relieve the clinging humidity. About two o'clock I checked my answering service, and I was asked to call Mr. Anderson at three, four, or five o'clock only. The name was new to me and the time scheme seemed a little nutty, but in my business you can never tell. So at three I dialed and a man's deep, grating voice answered.

"Mr. Anderson, this is John Foley."

"Mr. Foley, I have a job for you. Anderson isn't my name but Eric Fuller recommended you to me. I need help and you can set your fee within reason."

"Well, if Eric recommended me he probably told you I don't handle divorce work or anything like that."

"No, it's nothing in that line. But I have to find someone. Please come to the Manor Hotel at four. Don't ask for me. Take the elevator to the eighth floor, then take the stairs to the seventh floor. My room's seven-o-three. I'll be expecting you at four."

The last words were phrased with a tone of command, as though they came from a man used to giving orders and having them obeyed.

"Well, Mr. Anderson, I've just finished a case, and I don't think I want to take anything else on at the moment. But I can refer you to another good agency."

"No, Eric told me about you and gave you the highest praise. This is a missing persons case. It's my daughter and I've got to find her. She means more to me than anything in the world."

"Have you called the police? They have a good bureau for that sort of thing."

"I can't contact the police. There are too many other things at stake."

2

"OK. I won't promise anything but I'll be there at four and we can talk about it anyway."

I didn't want the job. But something about a man whose missing daughter meant everything and who wouldn't call the police when she was lost interested me.

I phoned Eric's office, but his secretary told me he would be in court for the rest of the day and couldn't be reached. So I changed into a fresh suit and reluctantly put on a shoulder holster. It's always better to be careful.

As I drove into the main part of the city, the hot moisture rolled in through the windows and up from the floor. I began to curse silently idiots who get melodramatic ideas during hot May days.

The Manor Hotel is a towering edifice on the main city square across from the City Hall. While much of its business has been lost to the new ersatz-modern motels in the suburbs, it still stands and dispenses the comforts of the twenties and thirties. On the way I took a circuitous route just to be sure I had no tail. As I went through the lobby, I couldn't identify any suspicious types, only the typical afternoon loungers in a hotel lobby.

I took the elevator to the second floor and made my way to a frosted-glass door with the legend SECURITY OFFICE. The tall blond receptionist was relaxed at the desk reading, oddly enough, *Playboy,* or maybe it wasn't so odd. She had to know what the competition was up to. She showed me back to Al Crawford's cubicle, and I interrupted him in his logkeeping. Al was an old cop who looked like a timid CPA. But he was careful, tenacious and discreet.

"Hi, John. What brings you around here?"

"Just between you and me, I'd like to know what you know about the guy in room seven-o-three."

"Seven-o-three's not a room, it's a suite, and the occupant is Frank McReedy, president of the International Dockman's Union. You don't know where you heard it, and I'd like to know if you have trouble in mind."

"No, I may do a job for him, that's all." So I told him the story as a reward for the information.

"Sounds screwy, John. But if you get wind of anything that could mean trouble here, let me know, will you?"

I assured him I would and headed back to the elevator bank.

My finger had hardly left the bell button for 703 when the door opened, disclosing a short, squat man, partially bald and with the hint of a paunch. He was probably in his late forties and his stance and the clarity of his gray eyes suggested a quiet toughness that was impressive.

"Mr. Foley?"

I nodded, and he motioned me inside. It was a well-appointed suite with sitting room, bedroom and bath. Against the far wall of the sitting room was a small but well-stocked portable bar. I was happy to feel the rather harsh air-conditioning.

Once inside, we shook hands and I felt a restrained force in his grip. He was in his shirt sleeves and slippers, but he wasn't relaxed.

"Look, Mr. Foley, I'm sorry for what you must think is a lot of folderol. But I'm in a sort of critical situation, and I have to take every precaution no matter how silly it may seem."

"That's all right. Those situations are my business."

"How about a drink before we start to talk?"

I agreed to a bourbon on the rocks, and he went quickly to the bar and poured Old Grand-Dad over ice for me and a ginger ale for himself. After he handed me my drink he sat opposite me, extended his legs and shook his head as though in a daze.

"To start with, my real name's Frank McReedy."

I gave no indication of either surprise or foreknowledge.

"The same McReedy who's head of the International Dockman's Union?"

"That's right. So you've heard of me, then."

I nodded.

"Officially and truly I'm here to consult with the international reps and local presidents. But there's something else even more important."

"You mentioned your daughter on the phone. She's missing. Is that it?"

"Yes, but I'd better give you all the background first so you'll know the whole situation."

"However you want to handle it. But, as I said, I won't guarantee that I'll take the job."

"OK, just hear me out." He frowned and took a sip of the ginger ale.

"What do you know about my union?"

"Not very much. Just what I've read in the papers. I know you've created a stir in Washington with civil rights demands."

"That's right. Well, myself and a few others, we made the Dockman's Union in the forties. We built it into a strong national organization with muscle. When we started there was nothing. But the UAW had made itself felt in autos and the way was open to organize."

He stopped and fidgeted around in the chair while sipping ginger ale.

"To make it short, by the fifties we were a power. A strike by us could tie up the entire country. So we got bigger and bigger and the ties between us and the rank and file became looser. I started as a socialist, and I still am. But hammering out contracts that cover an entire country doesn't give much leeway for idealism."

"How does all this affect your daughter?"

"Wait, we'll get to that." His voice took on a curt, autocratic tone to indicate that I was an underling who was out of line.

"Anyway, we've fought and won good wages and good working conditions. But with all of this, local affairs have turned up that aren't always easily dealt with on the level of the international. Wildcat strikes keep happening, and they're hard to handle.

"Too, it isn't always easy to keep social goals in line with economic goals. I've taken a stand on civil rights and we've set up a special fund to help. This comes out of dues and some of the membership isn't too happy. There's been a lot of stuff like this."

He reached into his shirt pocket and handed me a leaflet. It showed on the top a drawing of a Negro boy and a white girl walking hand in hand to a schoolhouse; below was a photo of a Negro man and a white girl dancing, with the legend "THIS IS WHAT MCREEDY WANTS." I shook my head and handed it back to him.

"I've seen stuff like this from Mississippi before."

He grimaced as he folded the leaflet and put it back in his pocket.

"But this doesn't come from the South. These have been given out by workers in Chicago, Detroit and here. Let's face it, my membership is not what you'd call enlightened. With this and the local issues problem, I could be in trouble when the next election for union president is held, in two months."

"I've heard you have some opposition."

"Right. Mike Cassidy is running on a reform slate. He's playing down the racism and claims to have nothing to do with this bilge." He tapped his shirt pocket.

"But he's tied in with it and he may even win. After that, if he does, I think he plans a tie-in with Pete Martin and the

6

Overland Haulers. You know how Martin runs things. He's a business-union man and only wants pay for his men and power for his union. However, power always comes first. Plus he has all sorts of racket and syndicate connections. Anyway, that's my situation. Now I've got another problem."

"And that's where I come in."

"Yes. I told you all of this so you'd know that discretion is essential in handling this. I don't want anything to get out. It could be harmful."

He fidgeted some more in the chair and then got up to refill his glass.

"Have another?"

"No, this is fine as it is. I can't promise anything. I'll protect a client's confidence as much as I can, but if a crime is involved there are limits. I won't try to cross those."

"Fair enough. I can't ask for anything more. Frankly, I don't know what you may be up against."

He walked over to a coffee table in the center of the room which had a slim leather portfolio on it. From this he took an envelope and moved back to his chair holding the envelope and then balancing it on his knee.

"My daughter's twenty years old. She's a junior at State U. here. She's a political science major and she's already planning graduate study at Berkeley. She spent two summers in Mississippi, and she's even part of a case that's going up to the Supreme Court."

"OK, but what about her disappearance?" He was perched on the edge of the chair in a certain eager pose that suggested he was reliving a lost youth.

"Wait, I'm getting to that. The past year or so she's been active in the protest movement against the war. I don't agree with her; I've made a public stand in support of the Administration's policy. But she's got a right to stand up for her own beliefs.

"Anyway, two weeks ago I got this letter and that's the last I've heard from her."

He handed the envelope across to me, and I took out a much-wrinkled typewritten sheet of blue stationery:

> DEAR DAD,
> I'm going away for a week or so. Please don't worry, but there is something I have to do.
>> Love,
>> GINNY

"When did you get this?"

"Two weeks ago; she sent it special delivery and we got it the next day."

"Did you try to call her or anything to find out what she might be up to?"

He shook his head and smiled with forced resignation as though I had asked a foolish elementary question.

"No, we've always trained Virginia to be a free agent and accept her own responsibilities."

"So what are you worried about, then?" I let disgust show in my voice. I was getting tired of McReedy's self-righteousness.

"Two weeks is a long time with no word. Frankly, she may be in trouble. The letter came just as I was on my way to New York. My wife and I were there for a week at a conference. When we got back we expected word, but there wasn't any. I called her landlady and told her Ginny would be gone for a while."

"Why did you do that?"

"Well, we didn't want any awkward questions asked. I checked with a few of her friends, but they had no idea where she might be."

He stood up and walked across the room to look out of the window and remained there for a while with his back turned.

"Could this be an abortion problem?"

"I don't think so. She would have discussed that with us and particularly with my wife, her stepmother."

"Where's her mother? Could she have gone to her?"

With this he turned to face me and remained standing with his back to the window.

"Her mother left me when Ginny was one year old. I have no idea what happened to her. Later I divorced her and married Irma, my present wife. For all intents and purposes, Irma is her mother."

"Well, how about her friends at school?"

"CeeJay Jones used to be her boyfriend."

"Is that the Negro civil rights leader?"

Once again he crossed to the chair opposite me and sat with his legs crossed and an expression of exasperation as he went through the details.

"Yes, she met him in Mississippi. He's older than she is, but his work prevented him from graduating. He's finishing his degree next month. Anyway, he's now working as what he calls a black revolutionary. I don't agree with him but that's a long story. Anyway, he and Ginny haven't seen much of each other in the last few months. But he knows nothing about her now. I also checked with Paul Howard, who's a philosophy professor there and a close friend. He says he thought she'd gone home to see us because she seemed to be pretty tired the past few days."

I could see clouds forming over the sky through the window, and I was beginning to feel pretty cloudy about the job I was being offered.

"OK, how do you want me to work?"

"I want her found, God damn it! I'm in a tricky enough spot now with this election and all the rest. Ginny's free to do as she wants, but I don't want something hitting me without knowing about it beforehand." He was leaning forward in the chair and his face was now contorted with annoyance.

"For a starter, I've already had one of my men check the hospitals and places like that. Nothing."

"That was a good idea." I tried not to let sarcasm appear in my voice.

"I expect you to handle this discreetly. If anything is seriously the matter, I want to know about it. I suppose Ginny may feel a little neglected by us in the past few years, but it's hard to manage everything."

"OK, I'll take the job at two hundred a day plus expenses and a thousand-dollar guarantee."

A few minutes later I was holding his check for a thousand dollars, along with a photo of a small-boned blond girl with straight hair. He was gesturing me to the door. He had also given me Ginny's address and her landlady's name.

"Don't contact me unless it's absolutely necessary. I'll be here for the rest of the week, but don't call me unless you have to. I'll call you and check."

"Just one more thing. Are there any relatives she may have gone to?"

"No. I have none, and my wife only has an aunt in California that Ginny never met."

When I reached the street, the clouds overhead had become sullen and looked ready to disgorge their contents. The city traffic was getting thick as the suburbanites fought their way back to their homes and hearths, to leave the center of town almost barren except for a few wanderers. I decided to skirt the traffic problem by leaving my car where it was and taking my chances with the rain. The heat was becoming even more oppressive as the storm drew nearer. However, it took only a few minutes to reach the public library and find help in its air-conditioning.

I made my way to the newspaper section, and I was soon seated with the past month's city papers in front of me.

CeeJay Jones and his local organization, SCRAP (Student Committee for Rehabilitation and Power), had received a wide but not particularly favorable press. Pieces abounded on its demands for cessation of the war and for power to the black community. Jones had built a group with two faces. On the one side were the predominantly white students in the university who insisted that government was following an imperialist foreign policy and using poor Negroes to enforce it. Then there was a small group of Negroes who called for various steps, ranging from the destruction of the city at the most extreme to a guaranteed income at the most conservative.

In the forefront of this was Jones, who led the groups in picketing, draft board disruption and speeches that seemed designed to panic the most liberal sections of the community. The more conservative were already demanding his arrest.

After returning the papers to the librarian, who regarded me suspiciously, I went to the card catalogue and looked for Paul Howard. The cards showed that he was born in 1930, and he was represented by three titles: *The Depersonalized Man in Our Time, The Phenomenology of Alienation,* and *Why Toleration?* I hunted through the shelves of the philosophy section and located copies of them, which I took with me.

The rain had come and gone, leaving the streets with slowly drying puddles, and there was a growing coolness in the air that was a relief. I retrieved my car and drove to Phillips' Restaurant, a short distance from my apartment. It took me a little over an hour to go through a martini and a lamb chop. At ten o'clock I turned into my garage.

Once inside, I made some coffee and turned the FM on low to a station playing Vivaldi. I started to glance through Howard's books and kept at it for the next couple of hours.

They were verbose with heavy Germanic sentences from which I learned that man in America is a lonely atom victimized by oppressive work which brutalizes his spirit. His leisure hours aren't much better, for he is played on by a mendacious press and cheap entertainment. As far as I could make out, all of this was to be remedied through control by thinkers who would return him to honest work and leisure with strict but necessary management.

Before I went to bed, I looked at the girl's photograph again. She looked sad even with a smile. She was pretty, but it was a rather poignant prettiness.

That night I dreamed she was chasing me through long, empty library stacks. I had Howard's books under my arm and she was trying to retrieve them.

2

~ VIRGINIA McREEDY lived as a roomer on Elm Lane, a short quasi-suburban street about a ten-minute walk from the State University. Appropriately enough, large elm trees stood in front of each of the neat, medium-size two-story houses that faced each other. It was about ten in the morning when I parked in front of the green and white shingled house that belonged to Virginia's landlady.

Mrs. Shaw came to the door after a short delay and ushered me into a large, neatly appointed living room dominated by a twenty-one-inch TV and great quantities of house plants placed in pots throughout the room. She was a neat small woman in her late fifties with shining alert eyes and bluish-tinged gray hair.

"Mr. McReedy phoned me this morning and said you would probably be out here to see me. My heavens, I hope there's nothing the matter. He told me a few days ago that Virginia was with him." Her voice was thin and a little irritated, but on the whole I didn't blame her.

"At the time he didn't think anything was the matter, and

he didn't want anyone to be alarmed needlessly." That seemed true enough, as far as it went.

"Well, I don't know what I can do to help you." Her voice became rather flat and emphatic.

"I just want to ask a few questions. When did you see Virginia last?"

"Oh, it was just two weeks ago, a Tuesday night. I'd just come back from shopping, about five o'clock, and I met Virginia coming down the stairs from her room with an overnight bag."

"Did she say anything as to where she was going?"

Mrs. Shaw was perched on the edge of an easy chair covered with a bright flower-patterned cloth. She got up and began to straighten a pile of magazines on the coffee table in front of where I was seated on the davenport.

"No, as a matter of fact she just brushed by me and went out the door. I saw her waiting at the corner by the bus stop, but I didn't pay any attention particularly." She finished her tidying and retook her chair.

"How long has Virginia lived here?"

"She's my first roomer. My husband died three years ago, and I decided to rent the large bedroom upstairs. Virginia moved in then and she's stayed except for the summers." Her tone of voice changed from irritation to complacency.

"I guess she was a good tenant, then?"

"Why, certainly," she said with the querulous note again.

"What I mean is she didn't cause any disturbance with her friends or anything like that?" Mrs. Shaw was beginning to tire me.

"Of course not. She took her meals out. I don't furnish those. Actually, she kept to herself most of the time. She didn't entertain here. Oh, sometimes Ellen Harris came to see her."

"Ellen Harris?"

"I don't know much about her. I think she's a graduate student at the university."

"How about boyfriends?"

"No, I wouldn't allow that sort of thing. Virginia may have gone to jail in Mississippi, but she wasn't one of those dirty, vulgar trollops you see around the campus." Her voice snapped this off in my face.

I asked Mrs. Shaw if I could see Virginia's room and she led me back to the hall and up a clean white-painted stairway to the second floor. Virginia lived in a large bedroom fitted out with a desk, phonograph, bed, dresser and easy chair. On the desk were a telephone and a note pad. There were papers and phonograph records strewn across the top of the desk. Books were tossed askew and at random in the bookcase next to the desk.

"I haven't touched anything in here since Virginia has been away. I've just done some cleaning and changed the bed." She looked at me as if I should take pride in her efforts.

I glanced through the records on the desk and noted the album covers. John Coltrane, the Beatles, the Jefferson Airplane, Prokofiev—it was a miscellaneous and rather odd collection with no discernible principle. The same was true of the books: Fromm, Kant, Rousseau, Camus, Eliot, Pound. The most interesting item was a penciled manuscript with the words "Clear Water" in ink on the side:

> They beat us in Mississippi,
> the rain fell,
> the sun beat,
> and they moved us
> around the cells—

The poem seemed left for completion. I asked Mrs. Shaw if the handwriting was Virginia's and she said it was. I glanced through the dresser drawers under the fervid eyes of Mrs. Shaw, but there was nothing to catch anyone's attention in the assortment of feminine apparel and accouterments.

"I'll take this with me," I said, indicating the incomplete poem, which I folded and placed in my billfold.

"Well, I don't know about that."

"I'll take full responsibility and you can tell Mr. McReedy all about it."

"No, no, Mr. McReedy said you could do as you wish with Virginia's things." She turned and waited for me to go through the door. All the way down the stairs I could feel her eyes probing the back of my neck.

In my relief at leaving Mrs. Shaw, I didn't even mind the chill damp air that had taken the place of yesterday's heat. I drove for a block and a half and then saw the mass of the university take form as a silhouette against the dark towering clouds in the west.

It looked like a miniature city, with the high-rise dormitories scattered about the campus and dominating the lower, more spread-out buildings that dotted the carpet of well-kept grass. There were cranes and bulldozers interspersed with the structures to mark out the construction of additional units. All in all, I suppose, it merited the term "complex" to describe its layout.

In back and on the side of the campus were parking lots, which were now loaded with cars of all sorts, from shining new American models to squat VWs and even a few motorcycles. I pulled up to one of the entrances, which was barred on both the incoming and outgoing lanes by flimsy gates that opened when you inserted a quarter on the inbound side.

It took me several minutes of driving through the black-topped lanes to find a slot for my car. Finally I managed to squeeze between a Japanese-made motor scooter and an oversize Detroit convertible with all the accessories. The place made me wish I owned some automobile stock, any kind.

I'd been on the campus a few times, but I didn't know enough about its intricacies to find anyone. So I stopped a book-laden coed with staring eyes and a yellow pant suit colored to challenge the grayness of the sky. She'd never heard of Paul Howard because she was a speech major, but she pointed out the main Administration Building, set, appropriately enough, in the middle of the campus.

It was a squat three-story structure whose neat rows of neon-light tubes shone through the windows. There was an information desk on the first floor with a long-haired teen-age boy, who told me Professor Howard's office was in the Frederick Taylor Humanities Hall, about a half mile away on the other side of the campus.

The Humanities Building was one of the oldest of the conglomeration. Its halls were paneled in old dark wood and the wooden stairs creaked slightly as you stepped on them. A directory by the door informed me that the Philosophy Department took up the third floor and that Howard's office was in room 304.

I was taking a chance that he was in, but to phone ahead might mean being put off. Room 304 was at the beginning of a dingy corridor in which the fluorescent lights had an anachronistic look.

I tapped lightly on the frosted-glass door.

"Come in."

As I stepped through the door I thought I was entering chaos. There were books and periodicals piled about the floor, overflow from the shelves, which were packed tight with printed matter. There was a desk with its back turned to the window, from which light came into the room. The desk too had its share of reading material, together with piles of what I took to be students' papers.

"Who the hell are you?" Howard was in a semireclining position in a rickety-framed swivel chair. His bushy black hair lorded over a round face with horn-rimmed glasses.

"I'm John Foley." I handed him a calling card, which he glanced at before dropping it on the desk.

"I'm working for Mr. McReedy, checking on his daughter's whereabouts."

"Oh, yeah, Virginia. He called me about her a week or so ago. I told him I hadn't seen her in a while, but I'd let him know if I did." His voice was low-pitched and forceful.

"Have you heard anything from her?" Without waiting for an invitation, I took a seat in a straight-back wooden chair set at an angle in front of the desk.

"No, if I had I'd have let him know, if Virginia wanted me to. By the way, I don't like cops, private or otherwise."

"That's your problem. But I'd appreciate whatever you could tell me about Virginia."

"How do I know if you're even working for McReedy?" He turned in the swivel chair and faced me, placing his hands together on the desktop.

I reached into my wallet and handed McReedy's check to him. He glanced at it, pursed his lips and whistled before giving it back to me.

"You guys are well paid," he snapped.

"The workman is worthy of his hire."

"OK, what can I tell you?"

"Oh, first generally about Virginia's general character. How did she impress you as a person?"

"She's a damned fine girl. You know she was in the South. They kicked the hell out of her down there, both physically and emotionally. Too, she's a very bright girl. I'm even letting her take my graduate seminar." He shifted back in his chair, propped his feet on the side of the desk and lit a cigarette. "Look, maybe I ought to put it this way. Virginia's part of the new generation. Our generation, you know, we copped out all along the line. Myself, for example. I've made graduate school, had some fellowships, knocked out a couple of books. But it hasn't been real. We've never touched the real world." He didn't seem to be talking to me; rather, his voice was addressed to an invisible class.

"Is that what you're getting at in your books?"

He leaned forward with a quizzical expression and stubbed out the cigarette in a glass ashtray. "You've read them?"

"Well, let's say I glanced through them. I don't much care about your style."

"Touché. But yes, I'm trying to discuss authentic humanity in a world that makes us inauthentic. We become liars, hypocrites, fascists, and all of this with a patina of liberalism that reeks of compromise."

"Is that the way Virginia thinks?" Howard was so engrossed in his exposition that my question caused his head to pull back sharply.

"For Virginia and the others, 'think' is probably too strong a verb."

"Well, feel, then, if that's any better."

"It is. They feel sold out, without any ground under their feet."

"What does that mean in terms of action for Virginia?"

He hesitated for a moment, made a church steeple of his hands and rested his chin on it.

"Virginia goes South, she fights there in the best way she can, and that means you lay your skin right on the line. Then you fight against war, imperialism and lying propaganda. What else can she do?"

"I don't know. I'm just trying to find out where she is."

"So the good liberal Frank McReedy can have a clear conscience and go on helping the proletariat?" His voice was a sneer.

Just as he heard the office door open, he dropped his feet and stood up. I half turned in my chair and saw a girl walk in and stand by my chair, facing Howard. She was tall with a good figure and dark-red hair. As far as I could guess, she was in her mid-twenties.

"Can't you even take the trouble to knock?" His tone and glance seemed calculatedly rude.

"I'm sorry. I know you're usually alone at this time of the day. I just thought I'd rush in and pick up the manuscript so I could work on it this afternoon."

"OK. OK." He silently refused to make any introductions.

He ruffled through some papers on the desk, and not finding what he wanted, probed into one of the bottom drawers of the desk. She reached across and took the fifty or so manuscript pages that he handed to her. Then she started to turn.

"Wait, Ellen. Here are some notes to be added." Some more pages were passed.

"Where are you going now?" The question was peremptory.

"I'm going to get some lunch at the Union, and then I have to take Sibyl's class at one-thirty."

"Will you be seeing her?"

"I don't think so. She said yesterday she wouldn't be around all day. She may be in the library for research."

"Well, if you do see her, tell her that I won't be home until late and ask her to call me." He finished the sentence in a tone of dismissal.

The girl held the papers against her breast and left the room, shutting the door with exaggerated care. Howard replaced his feet on the side of the desk and acknowledged my presence again.

"Where were we?"

"How has Virginia acted lately? Did she seem different in any way?"

"Virginia has always been a quiet girl. The two summers in Mississippi didn't change her much. Lately she's become something of a recluse."

"Any reason for it?"

"I think her break with CeeJay Jones, the Negro leader, may have had something to do with it. They were in the South together and until last fall they were very close."

"Were they lovers?"

"I don't know, but would it upset your cop's sensibility if they were?" The sneer was palpable in his eyes and mouth.

"I don't feel anything about it one way or the other. I just want to find the girl."

"So I suppose they were. She was around his apartment a lot. I think she may have helped him out with money. Things are pretty tight for him."

"Why did they break up?"

"I have no idea. Frankly, it's none of my business. They're both mature enough."

"Well, how is her course work?"

He leaned forward on the desk and glanced through the papers in front of him. I could see that he was trying to think up a good excuse to throw me out of the office.

"I know it's none of my affair. But frankly, I'm casting around. I haven't an idea about where the girl is. Hell, I've never even set eyes on her." I was getting a little annoyed at the whole thing myself.

He fumbled through some papers; all the while he kept his eyes away from me as though there were things of much greater importance in the papers. Maybe there were.

"I can't say about her other courses. But in my seminar—it's on Perception and Community if that means anything to you —her work has become increasingly erratic. The students have to write a short paper every week. Hers have become wilder and wilder. She wrote the last few in aphorisms. Brilliant, some of them, but not always to the point. Even a little cynical."

"Cynical in what way?"

"To put it as simply as I can, Virginia used to feel—it was one of the things that made my wife and me interested in her —that human community in peace and honesty was a possible thing."

"She doesn't now?"

"I don't know. I talked with her when she had dinner with us a few days before she disappeared. She was beginning to feel that we're all, in some degree, naturally corrupt." Here he paused to shake his head in simulated disgruntlement.

"Does this change your opinion of her?"

"Not really. Doubts are only a natural thing."

I stood up to leave. "Well, if you hear anything about her or if she gets in touch with you, I'd appreciate a call."

"Only if Virginia wants it. After all, she's a person in her own right, and I wouldn't want to go against her wishes."

It was only twelve-fifteen as I walked across the campus. But with both Howard and Mrs. Shaw under my belt, I felt as though I had worked a full day. I strolled through masses of students of all sorts. Some were attired like conventional high school kids of any generation. Here and there, scattered throughout the milling groups, were the beards, lanky straight hair and apparently grimy uniforms of the disaffected. In front of the Administration Building, a group of long-haired boys and their feminine twins were marching, carrying placards with slogans like: ADMINISTRATION FINKS OUT ON WAR and FEED DON'T BOMB.

The Student Union stood adjacent to a crane, which was engaged in digging up large clumps of red clayey earth. A sign indicated that the new medical school would be erected on the site. I went into the lobby of the Union and was greeted by a rock 'n' roll group chanting a plaintive lament about the failure of universal love. I walked down a corridor, following the arrow that pointed to the cafeteria. Book stalls and posters lined the hall, with students browsing and chatting.

The cafeteria was crowded. I glanced around the room and located the red-haired girl from Howard's office. Fortunately she was seated alone at a table for two in a back corner of the room. She seemed to be concentrating intensely on the meal in front of her.

I went to the counter that dispensed coffee for those who wanted to skip the lunch line. Holding my cup precariously in one hand, I pushed my way through the tables and students to the girl's corner. She looked up with a blank stare as I stood over her, as if I had interrupted her in something of great importance.

"Mind if I join you?"

"If you want to." There was no particular feeling of any sort in the answer.

"I'm John Foley."

"So what!"

"I was in Howard's office when you came in. Would you be Ellen Harris by any chance?" So far the conversation sounded like tired comedy patter in my ears.

"That's right. What's that got to do with you?" Her green eyes took on a hostile cast.

I handed her one of my cards, which she read with a disdainful expression before dropping it by the side of her coffee cup.

"I'm trying to find Virginia McReedy. I'm working for her father."

"Well, I haven't seen Virginia in over two weeks. Howard said something about her father's trying to find her. But it's none of my business."

"Her landlady said you were good friends."

"So, what she does with her life is no concern of mine. If she wants to get away for a while, why should I get upset." It wasn't a question, just a flat statement of conviction.

"Well, was she upset about anything when you last saw her? Had she any reason in particular to want to leave?"

"We all have problems, don't we." Again she spoke with only flat assertion, nothing else.

"What's your job here?"

"Not that it's any affair of yours, but I'm Sibyl Howard's teaching assistant in the Sociology Department."

There were folding chairs scattered around, with empty pop bottles and beer cans heaped in a pile in a corner. In the middle of the room, at the back, stood a battered desk. Over the desk, casting a malevolent glow against the blackened windows, a light bulb hung from a socket that dangled from the ceiling.

Two men sat by the desk in laughing conversation when I walked in. The one nearest me, a tall man with a green cloth cap on his head, started up and began to move toward me.

"I'm looking for CeeJay Jones." I could feel the hostility in the answering looks. The seated man stood up and motioned the other back. He was medium in height with light-brown skin and kinky hair that was kept short and close to his scalp. His eyes were bright and seemed lit with intensity.

"Yes, suh, boss. You done found him. What can this heah poor darkie do for you?" He shuffled my way, stopping for a moment to snatch the cap from the other man; the cap was held dangling in his left hand while he extended the right to me.

I ignored the proffered hand and stepped back to sit down in one of the folding chairs, which creaked under me. It was a volatile situation. Anything I did would probably be wrong. That didn't remove the necessity to do something anyway.

"Can we stop the minstrel show?" It sounded silly in my own ears.

"Heh, heh, now. Man says we not serious. But we's polite, boss." He was standing over me, and he moved to push me over backward. I stood up quickly and pushed him to the side; at the same time I unbuttoned my coat so the shoulder holster showed.

"Why, lookee here, the man's fuzz. He's done come down to crack our heads. Unless we crack his first." With the last

27

sentence, his pronunciation changed and his voice became soft but resonant.

"I'm private and I'm working for Virginia McReedy's father. I want to find her."

I kept my hands at my sides, hoping their trembling didn't show. He shrugged and sat on the top of his desk, swinging his feet. His friend sat down again, watching me. Jones gestured with his head in the direction of the door. The other man got up and retrieved his cap from the side of the desk before going out.

"OK, just who are you?" Jones stopped moving his feet and concentrated his gaze directly on me. I turned and sat down again.

"I'm John Foley." I passed out another calling card.

Jones studied it for a moment and then put it into his shirt pocket.

"I haven't seen Virginia more than two or three times since the first of the year, and then only for a few minutes." His tone was now as steady as his gaze.

"You used to be pretty close, weren't you?"

He leaned his head back and laughed. "Yeah, you could say that all right."

He sprang off the desk, paced back and forth across the room and returned to sit down in a chair facing me. Then he leaned forward and tapped my knee with two fingers.

"We were close. I met Virginia when we were both registering voters in Mississippi. Morning Star, Mississippi, of all the God-damned holes. I was dumb enough then to think we could make this society work, if we just got the votes." He leaned back in the chair and folded one leg over the other.

"I'm not too concerned with philosophy at the moment."

"My philosophy!" He gave an abrupt snort. "There wasn't

any philosophy when those cracker mothers began to break our heads."

"True enough. But I need to know about Virginia."

"She was there. That night they herded all of us off to jail. The women they dumped in one bullpen, the men in another. No miscegenation, dig?" His eyes never moved from my face, as though he hoped to see me disintegrate under the force of his scorn.

"Then they'd take some of us out in the back and work us over for a while. The brave, gallant honkies."

"OK, you've made the point."

"No, I haven't made any point. You want Virginia because that lily-white liberal father of hers is paying you. You don't see anything further than his bank account."

"Well, I'm sure as hell not going to see his daughter, talking to you." I got up and started to walk to the door.

"Wait. If I knew anything about her now, I'd tell you. But I don't. I thought at first she just wanted to be alone for a while; I guess she's been gone too long, though."

I wheeled around and stood in front of him. "Why'd you quarrel?"

"That's personal, cracker, and I'm not dragging my life out for you to spit at."

"I couldn't care less about your life." I was getting tired of the whole business.

"Let's say we just didn't see things the same way anymore."

"Was the breakup your idea or hers?"

He sat still for a moment and then stood up. His hand struck me flat on the shoulder with full force. I staggered a bit, but he made no move to follow up the blow.

"Get out of here, you mother. Get out the door and never let me see your stinking white skin around here again." He took a seat behind the desk and started to read a pamphlet.

When I got to the sidewalk, Trench Coat and Green Cap were talking and laughing at the side of the store. They followed me down the street, but turned off when I got into the car. I felt weary and hungry.

3

✍ IT BEGAN to rain as I drove into the main city. I didn't seem to be making any progress other than to be extremely unpopular with everyone I talked to. Watching the water being cut by the wipers, I reflected on the irascibility of everyone connected with the job. Since I hadn't seen my office in a week, I decided to check in there and hide from the rain and people.

However, a short survey through my rear-view mirror prevented me from taking a direct route. The car was a blue Chevrolet of early-sixties vintage, but the rain was too heavy and the sky too dark for me to make anything of the occupants. I debated on letting them waste their time following me, but I was also angry enough to want to annoy them. I made a quick left at a crowded light, which left them stranded as cars piled through the straightaway. Half a block later, I cut through a narrow alley onto the street with my office building on it. After parking and getting soaked between car and building, I made it into the lobby, tired and disgusted.

On my way to the elevator, I picked up a sandwich and milk with the early edition of the evening paper at the newsstand. My office was quiet enough to relieve some of the day's tension. I checked with the answering service and they told me Ellen Harris had called and would call back. There was nothing else other than a call from a lady who wanted someone to find her lost Pekingese. I decided not to return that call.

I ate the dry sandwich and sipped the milk through a straw while glancing through the carnage of the day in the papers. Roger Boyd's labor column contained an item of interest under the heading "LABOR JOTTINGS":

Mike Cassidy, Eastern regional vice-president of the International Dockman's Union, is putting his campaign against Frank McReedy into high gear. Cassidy charges McReedy has no interest in the laborers' problems; he cares only for power in Washington.

McReedy's forces are replying by showing how wages have risen under McReedy.

By the way, how about that secret meeting between Cassidy and Pete Martin in Vegas last week? Are they playing footsie or do they mean business?

When the telephone rang, I hoped it wasn't the lady with the missing Peke.

"Hi! Is this Foley the great detective?" Her voice on the phone was soft and rather husky. She didn't sound at all like the rather disgruntled girl I had spoken with earlier.

"Yes. Is this Miss Harris?"

"It's Mrs. Harris, not that that's important now. By the way, are you married?"

"No, I've never even tried it once."

"You're smart. Anyway, I'd like to see you sometime this evening, if I can. I really wasn't very fair with you this morning, and I'd like to apologize. Besides, there are a couple of things you probably should know about Virginia."

"Swell. Where can I see you?"

tense. She leaned forward and placed her drink on the coffee table in front of her.

"My husband's not here. I haven't seen him in a year." Some of her earlier hostility returned to her voice.

"I'm sorry. None of my business."

"That's right. But you don't have to be sorry. It doesn't make any difference now."

She picked up her drink and we sat for the next few moments in silence while she twisted the glass around in her hands.

"My husband's in a private sanitarium in California. His parents take care of him financially and they pay me to stay away." It was a flat declaration.

"That's still no affair of mine."

"No reason you shouldn't know. We were married in our junior year at Santa Maria College. He was in philosophy, I was in sociology. We were both very bright, and I guess we were in love."

She lapsed into silence and I used the interval to freshen my drink.

"His parents have money. His father runs one of those small electronics firms that make a lot of money out there. They despised me."

"Why?"

"They would have hated anyone who took their boy. And my folks have no money. Dad's a buyer in a department store out there. I was a scholarship student."

"What happened?"

"David was one of the earliest heads. That's what happened. After several trips he had a complete breakdown. I guess that's the polite way to put it."

"You're talking about LSD?"

"That's right. You see, we took part in the demonstration at Santa Maria for a free life. After that died down, we found acid."

"We?"

"Oh, sure. I tried it once and all I got was scared, so scared I thought I'd rather be dead." The fear was still there, for her face was contorted with anxiety.

"What about your husband?"

"Well, for him it was a great experience. He said it taught him how wonderful life could really be. He kept on, and then just after graduation we took a vacation in Acapulco. I came back to the hotel one day and he was sitting in the middle of the floor with no clothes on. Then he started to scream." Her shoulders began to shake and she buried her face in her hands, with her elbows on her knees. The sobbing seemed to wrench her whole body.

I left her to cry it out while I went to the kitchen and put on some coffee. By the time I brought it back, she was wiping the remnants of the tears from the corners of her eyes, with a lace handkerchief.

"I'm sorry to break down like that, but I haven't had anything to eat since lunch. I guess the drink got to me." She took the coffee I had placed on the table and moved her drink to the other side.

"Liquor and sadness usually don't meet," I said.

"Anyway, David cracked completely. His parents had him put away under private care. I got the blame from them. But they made me a deal. I go away and stay away for a definite sum each month. So here I am." She shrugged her shoulders and smiled at me with a twist of the head.

"How does your husband feel about the arrangement?"

"I don't know. I never want to hear of him again."

"You sound as though he did everything just to spite you."

"No, I know I can't blame him. It's just that I have had enough of the whole scene. Drugs, protest, all the rest. I don't want any more." She seemed drained of energy as she leaned back against the cushions.

"So I came on here. I got a teaching fellowship in the Sociology Department. Now I'm the great Mrs. Howard's teaching assistant. That means I do all the work while she finishes her book. Then I help type her husband's stuff to make ends meet. I may be a remittance girl, but David's family only pays me off to the tune of a hundred a month." She pursed her lips together and shook her head back and forth while she swallowed the coffee.

"Does the whole Howard family write?"

"Sure. They're big in the anti-Establishment Establishment. Fellowships, sabbaticals, all the trimmings, so they can tell the donors just how rotten they are."

She stopped talking to lean down and slip her high-heeled shoes off. Then she swung her feet under her and pulled at the skirt to make it cover her knees. It didn't.

"How did Virginia McReedy figure in all of this?"

"I met her for the first time last September at a party the Howards gave for some of their grad students. She was there with CeeJay Jones. They were very close then. Say, could I have another cup of coffee?"

While I was pouring the coffee in the kitchen, she continued talking.

"I didn't get to know Virginia very well at all then. I used to see her in Mrs. Howard's office sometimes. Mrs. Howard's book is on the sociology of stress, and Virginia used to give her case histories from Mississippi."

"What was the relationship between CeeJay and her?" I put a fresh cup of coffee on the table for her.

"I don't know for sure. I guess she was sleeping with him. It was sort of taken for granted." She patted the seat next to her to indicate it wouldn't be unwelcome if I sat there. I went back to the easy chair.

"Where would they go? Mrs. Shaw says she didn't bring any men around to her place, and I heard CeeJay lives with his mother."

"Yes, he does, but he has a separate section of her house all to himself, with his own entrance. I was at a party there once with some of the Howards' students."

"Are the Howards friendly with CeeJay?"

"Yes and no. But the black problem isn't the only thing they're interested in. They want something they call a spiritual revolution. Hell, all CeeJay cares about is to see the blacks take over." She stretched her legs out the length of the sofa and concentrated her gaze on her toes, which she curled and uncurled as she talked. They were nice legs.

"I take it Virginia was in sympathy with these things."

"When I first knew her, she was, very definitely. But that was a few months before CeeJay became really outspoken on black power."

"What happened then? From what I've heard about her, I would think she'd be in favor of it."

She sat up abruptly and rested her stocking feet on the floor. After two sips of the coffee, she leaned back and folded her hands demurely in her lap.

"She was, but by then she'd done some thinking too. I think she started to see everything is a fight, a battle for power."

"I'm not sure I understand."

"She started to think that CeeJay was right and the Howards also. But in the end they'd be just as bad as the ones in power now. At least I think that's what she meant."

"How did you learn all this?"

"Around the first of the year she stopped seeing much of either CeeJay or the Howards. We ran into each other here and there. Then she started dropping by my place or I'd stop in at hers." She sat looking at me steadily as her fingers began to pick at the paper napkin I'd placed on the table for her.

"I guess my experiences with David made her feel I'd understand."

"Did you tell her about it all?"

"No, she already knew. I'd made the mistake of telling Sibyl Howard. So of course she told Virginia. You know, she's really a bitch. Pretty and very, very competent. But at heart, pure bitch of the first quality." Her shoes were back on and she was playing with the strap of her handbag. I didn't know if she really wanted to go or whether she was just playing a game.

"What about Virginia's disappearance?"

"Really, I don't know anything. At first I thought she might just be tired. But she's been gone too long now without some word."

"Could she have been suicidal?"

"Oh, I don't think so. She's much too levelheaded a girl to go off that way. The last time I saw her she didn't seem depressed."

"When was that?"

"Let's see. It was on Friday night. We had dinner at the Union and then went to a movie."

"Was there anything at all unusual in her behavior?"

She looked down at the rug for a moment in thought. "No,

39

nothing to indicate she was thinking of going away. She did ask me about my mother."

"What about her?"

"Oh, she wanted to know how well I knew her and if she meant much to me."

"Was that all?"

"Well, she went on to say that she'd never known her own mother and that while her stepmother had always been good to her, she couldn't help wondering about her natural mother. That's about all. I told her about my mother being just a regular housewife and that sort of thing."

She stood and picked up the coffee cup and saucer. "May I look at your kitchen? I'd like to see how a detective lives."

I nodded and followed her in. She placed the cup in the sink and washed it out.

"You're a very considerate guest."

She turned and brushed past me, back to the living room. "Not really. I'm just lonely, to be honest. You interested me this afternoon. So with my curiosity to be satisfied, I called you." She took a seat in my easy chair, kicked off her shoes again and stretched her legs out.

"Do you always go around in your stocking feet?"

"Sure, doesn't everyone?"

"Tell me more about Virginia."

"Don't you ever stop working? Here I am practically telling you I like you and all you want is information." With this she shrugged her shoulders, got into her shoes and went over for her handbag.

"I'm a detective. It's my business to ask questions. Besides, we don't live in the same neighborhoods. You wouldn't like my kind of person."

"If you say so. But I'm awfully weary of the sort of people who do live in my neighborhood." After a moment's hesitation, she sat on the edge of the sofa and moved her bag onto her knees. I busied myself with another drink.

"What's the matter with the people you know?"

"They're bright, smart and a pain in the rear end. It's just personality, and personality is always beating on you. Everyone's got to be smarter than everyone else."

"You sound embittered. How old are you anyway?" I stood in front of the coffee table as she got up and moved toward the door.

"Twenty-three, and I'm not really bitter about anything. Just realistic."

I started to follow her to the door. Then she turned to face me.

"So I'll have to ask you."

"Ask me what?"

"Take me to dinner, and I'll show you how they live in my circles." She was smiling with both her mouth and her eyes. It struck me that she was a remarkably good-looking girl. I felt like an aging lecher.

"Where do you want to go to dinner?"

"I'm through tomorrow afternoon at six. You meet me in the coffee room at the Union, and we'll take it from there."

I agreed. After she had gone I sat for a few minutes in thought about the possible misadventures of a twenty-three-year-old graduate student and a much older private detective. It seemed too incongruous for much serious consideration.

I went to the kitchen and made myself a corned beef sandwich and some more coffee. As I was eating, I reread the poem I had taken from Virginia McReedy's room. When this yielded

41

nothing in the way of insight, I studied her photograph for a few moments; but the captured face refused to relinquish anything helpful.

Afterward I hauled out my U.S. atlas and searched Mississippi for a town or waterway named Clear Water. Again I came up with a blank. Neither the state nor any area close by had such a name listed. From a day's arduous legwork I had got nothing that offered an obvious lead. McReedy's money seemed badly spent. I considered just tossing in the towel on the case, but that seemed pointless too.

4

◜ I WAS awakened at eight in the morning by the insistent ringing of the telephone. When I answered, it was McReedy to check on my progress. My lack of achievement didn't sit too well with him. I considered again giving up the job. McReedy was a jumpy client, and I don't like that kind. Finally I compromised with myself and agreed to meet him that afternoon at three in a bar and restaurant near his hotel.

The thought of taking a couple of weeks' vacation if I quit took up most of my attention while I fixed myself bacon and eggs. Of course, McReedy could always use the police or another detective. Maybe Virginia was another Judge Crater.

I was halfway through my second cup of coffee when my buzzer rang. When I went to the house phone, I was answered by CeeJay Jones' voice asking to come up.

"OK. Just a minute." I released the entrance door and went to the bedroom and put on my bathrobe. As a precaution I dropped my gun into the pocket. After a minute Jones' knock came at the door.

He was dressed in a dark-gray suit complete with vest. He was the image of the cliché Madison Avenue type.

"Well, where's your goon squad this morning?" I didn't think there was any need to be cordial.

He didn't reply at first, just walked into the room and casually surveyed the furniture before taking a seat in my easy chair and crossing his legs.

"Very nice how you white folks live." The twist of sarcasm was back in his voice again.

"Can it, will you! It's early and I'm still tired. What the hell do you want?"

I leaned against the wall by the door and watched him while he laughed in a series of short snorts.

"Right, baby. Look, I really came to apologize. I didn't send those brothers after you. I didn't even know about it until late last night. Then I practically blasted them out of the movement." He looked directly at me and from his expression of unease I could sense sincerity.

"How did they find out where I live?"

"That was my fault, man. After you shook their tail, they came back to the center, but I was gone. I'd tossed your calling card in the desk and they found it. That's all."

"So why did they want to work me over?"

"They're new to the movement, and they're in the indiscriminate-violence bag, dig? You were bugging me about some gray chick, that's all they knew. So they tried to jump you."

"So now you've apologized and all's right with the world. How would you feel if those idiots had beaten my head in?" I had to restrain myself from an anger that made me want to go over and clout him. Instead I went across the room and sank down on the sofa.

"Well, you honkies have clobbered enough of us niggers. It would have just been too bad." He edged around on the chair to start to leave.

"Wait a minute. Let's even things up by talking about Virginia McReedy. Remember, that's what started all this."

"Yes, yes." He leaned back in the chair and gave a theatrical sigh. "Go ahead and ask your questions," he said.

"Why did you break up with her?"

"You're getting sort of personal, aren't you?" He was grinning now with a certain sardonic satisfaction.

"Her father feels it is a personal thing."

"Why, bless good Daddy McReedy. I wouldn't want to worry him so that he be so upset he couldn't make any more civil rights stands. We darkies need him."

"Fine. If all you can do is put on this act, then get the hell out of here. As far as I can see, the best thing Virginia ever had happen to her was to be dumped by you." My anger was only partially put on for the occasion. In truth CeeJay Jones was becoming one of nature's great bores for me.

"I dumped her! Man, is that what you think? Why, you're even dumber than I thought any honkie could be." Now he dug his shoulders into the back of the chair and put his hands on the arms as though preparing for a long stay. He started his snorting laughter again.

"You're all wrong, baby. You wouldn't know, but she was my wife." His antagonistic tone became more straightforward.

"When were you married?"

"It was this way. We went back South together last summer. You know, by that time most of the do-gooding gray boys and girls were starting to stay home. Well, we wanted to form our own party in Mississippi. Hell, all we got was broken heads again." Now he wasn't really addressing me; he was just talking into the air.

"So we got back here at the end of August. Soon as we did,

45

we took off again for a few days and got married. We took a week's honeymoon at Shadow Lake, downstate."

"Why did you keep it secret?"

"She wanted it that way. Not that she cared about the color thing. But she thought people in the movement here might take it out on me for marrying a white. I guess she was right. But hell, she isn't white, she's human." He began to take account of me again and started to study my face for some reaction. I didn't think there was any there.

"Anyway, we hung out together and I'd take her to my place a couple of times a week. But then everything fell apart."

"What happened?"

"I don't know exactly," he said. Then he relapsed into silence for several moments while I waited, not caring to prod him any further.

"About Thanksgiving she started to talk about how we'd made a mistake. Don't get me wrong—we still loved each other and there wasn't anyone else for either of us."

As he went on, the hostility left his face and speech completely. The hip talk was also absent. He was just a man remembering.

"But Virginia had started to rethink everything. Finally she said I belonged with my people and not with her. She was white and couldn't help it, but there it was. We had to separate—or so she said."

"That was pretty extreme, wasn't it?"

"I thought so. I still do. But no, for her that's the way it had to be and nothing less would do."

"Did she want a divorce?"

"No. She said we'd wait and see. And then she started to tell me about how we were the underdogs, but when we won

46

we'd be just another group with power. For me she'd be just a handicap and one day I'd realize it and hurt her."

"So she hurt you first?"

"No, that wasn't it. I know she wasn't trying to hurt me. Only to help me and the cause. You know, it's serious business. We're not fooling."

I nodded my head in agreement. He took another pause and knotted his fists on the arm of the chair.

"Anyway, that's what happened."

"Didn't you try to talk her out of it?"

"Sure, sure. But she can be a very determined girl."

"Did you see her at all after this happened?"

"Oh, we ran into each other from time to time. But she started to treat me like a stranger."

"Was she still involved in civil rights work on her own?"

"Not directly. She shifted to antiwar activity. But even then, as far as I know, she didn't get too involved." He waited in silence like a witness on the stand.

"Well, surely you must have tried to see her. You couldn't have just taken it and forgotten all about it."

"Look, man, I'm telling it to you like it happened. Or can't you whiteys believe anything?" All of his old anger returned as he contemptuously shook his head and stood up to go.

"Look, I'm a busy man. If she doesn't want me, well, I'll manage. Just gives me that much more time to work on you honkies." He was halfway to the door with his back turned to me.

"Just one more question," I said.

"What?" He turned and crossed his arms in front of his chest.

"Did she ever say anything about her mother?"

"No, just that she'd never known her. She'd left while Ginny was a baby. Anything else, gray boy?" He spat out the last.

When I shook my head no, he went out fast and slammed the door with full force.

It was late in the morning before I got to my office. The unseasonable heat had returned and the sun shone mercilessly on the car hood as I made my way through the traffic. Actually I could as well have stayed home for all the leads I had. But I thought I might at least stop at the office and check the morning mail.

When I got to the office door I stepped back quickly so my shadow wouldn't appear on the frosted-glass door panel. For as I had reached for my keys, the clanging sound of a desk drawer being slammed reached me from inside.

Keeping myself carefully to one side, I inserted the key and stepped into the side of the anteroom with my gun drawn. Behind my desk in the main room a chubby red-haired man sat up with a start and pulled back in my chair.

"Hold it and keep your hands flat on the desk!" I said as I moved into the room. He did as I said, and I was surprised to see his face flush like the legendary Victorian maiden's.

"I can explain," he said.

"I bet you can," I retorted. I kept the gun steady. "So start."

His hand moved to his upper jacket pocket very slowly. From it he took a small leather card case, which he flipped across the desk so that it landed at my feet.

I stepped into the room and moved to the far side, still holding the gun on him. "OK, get up now and hand it to me. Don't be in a hurry."

He did as I said and he was a study in slow motion. I flipped the case open with my left hand and saw him identified as

Special Agent Charles O'Connor. It didn't take a minute to toss the case at his feet and shove him back forcibly into the client's chair at the side of my desk. The sides of the chair creaked as his substantial form hit it. I went and took my seat behind the desk and put the gun away. He retrieved his case shamefacedly and sat up to face me.

"So how come the government's interested in the contents of my desk? I take it for granted you didn't bother with a warrant."

"If you'll calm down for a minute I'll explain." He spoke in a voice that sounded as though he were huffing and puffing rather than talking. I leaned back in my chair and waited.

"We heard you were checking on CeeJay Jones. All we wanted was to see what you were up to. You know we consider him a very dangerous man."

"If you wanted to know something, you could have asked me. If you wanted to search my office, you could have got a warrant."

"Listen, this is government business. Where do you get the idea some cheap private eye can tell us what to do?" His tone was now bristling and belligerent.

"So I'm just supposed to sit still while you walk all over me and my business?"

He sneered as though he enjoyed the idea of power. "Someday your license will be up for renewal. It can be seen to that you'll never get it here or anywhere else."

"Suppose you get out of here right now. If you and your people want to make trouble, start it. I have nothing to say about myself or my clients or my business without a subpoena."

He hesitated before starting to rise; then he sat down again. "Wait a minute, don't get in a lather. We know you're looking for the McReedy girl. Is it a snatch?"

"If it were, you'd be in on it. Come on, your undercover boys in Jones' setup know better than that." I waited, but he maintained silence with an abashed look. For a minute I was afraid he'd cry.

"My guess is your timing is off. I'll bet this search was something you were supposed to pull last night but you didn't. What'd you have to do, take your wife out?"

He jumped up and stood in front of the desk with rage apparent in his grimace.

"I'll fix you, gumshoe. You make any complaint about this and we'll hound you to hell and back."

"Maybe you'd better sit down, then, and tell me about CeeJay."

"What do you mean?"

"What's so special that you need to check everything like this?"

He took his seat and lit a cigarette with hands that were not too steady. "We have to. You've heard some of the things he's said, haven't you? It's our job to check that kind of thing."

"Even if you break the law while you're doing it?" My question was rhetorical.

He smiled again. "If that guy starts killing people and burning them out, nobody's going to care."

"Well, he hasn't so far. Until he does or you have some evidence he's going to do so, stay away from me or I'll make some trouble of my own."

"Nobody will listen to you, buddy. Nobody at all. If somebody did, it's easy to denounce them and you as kooks. Now you're wasting my time." He pulled himself erect and literally stalked out of the office.

As soon as I got my anger under control, I called Eric Fuller's office. He's a criminal lawyer and a good one. I'd done several jobs for him in the past and he'd helped me a couple of times. When I got hold of him, he suggested we meet for lunch at his club, near the Courthouse.

I made the mistake of walking it. By the time I made the vestibule of the club, I felt like someone emerging from a Turkish bath. Eric was waiting for me at a corner table in the expansive dining room. He is a tall, thin man in his late thirties with a completely bald head. His appearance was dominating, as many of the D.A.'s men had discovered when they met him in court.

"Hi, John, how's the snooping?" His cordiality is as imposing in private as his belligerency is in court. While we had a drink and ordered lunch, I described my encounter with Charles O'Connor.

"Say, you do stir up more trouble, John!"

"Yeah, thanks to the jobs you drum up for me!"

"Seriously, I don't think you have too much to worry about from Mr. O'Connor. You know, you may be right that he was supposed to have done the job in the night. Those guys get pretty careless sometimes."

"Yes, but just because someone blunders doesn't mean I'm completely covered."

"That's true," he said. He paused for a moment and studied the olive in the bottom of his martini. "You know, in this town probably even the newspapers wouldn't want to go up against their organization."

"I figured that."

"But still, when they fumble around like this they don't like to take any chance that there'll be a complaint. After all, they haven't had too good a press in some areas recently. Besides, I have some connections and I can put some pressure on if I have to. Don't worry about it."

"I won't," I said. "That's what I pay you for."

We concentrated on the food for the next few minutes. Finally I broached the main reason for my calling him.

"What about McReedy, Eric?"

"He's a damn fine man, John. Really, he's one of the best I know."

"How well do you know him?"

He didn't answer for a time but gestured for the waitress to bring us coffee.

"Oh, I did some work for him about ten years ago during an organizing campaign here in the city. I've done a few jobs since then from time to time."

"Why did he need a criminal lawyer?" I asked.

"During the Meecham strike a few years ago a couple of stewards were charged with assault in a picket line fight. I got them off."

"Were they guilty?"

"Let's just say it was a pretty nasty strike on both sides and let it go at that." He retreated to his plate.

"Did he tell you about the job I'm doing for him?"

"Sure. He came to see me as soon as he got to town and asked who I'd recommend for that sort of work. Of course I said you."

I told him how McReedy had outlined the case for me. Eric nodded his head over his coffee cup.

"Yes, that's just about what he told me. I hope you can turn up something. He's worried stiff, you know. He told me it takes about three pills to get him to sleep since she's been gone."

"Do you know Virginia at all?"

"Oh, a couple of years ago he brought her along to lunch with us. Right here, as a matter of fact."

"What kind of girl is she?"

"Shy, pretty, very intense and tremendously fond of her father, as far as I could see."

"How about Virginia's mother?"

"All I know is she left him after Virginia was born. Irma, her stepmother, is a good woman. She used to be McReedy's secretary before they were married."

"Was that why the first Mrs. McReedy went away?"

"No, there's nothing there for you. Irma didn't start to work for him until after he was deserted. You know, the people we come into contact with certainly make cynics of us." He pushed back his chair a bit and looked at me with a half smile, half grimace.

"Still, I've got to find out what kind of person I'm working for. You know that as well as anyone," I countered.

"So stop worrying. You've got a client who's a first-rate man in all respects." He waved at the waitress to bring the check.

5

~⊙ I WAS a few minutes early for my appointment with McReedy, so I took a corner table at the back of the bar and glanced through an evening paper while I waited. McReedy was prompt and I had hardly got beyond the front page when I saw him coming across the room. He sat down and ordered a ginger ale again while I stuck with bourbon and water.

"Have you come up with anything yet, Foley?" he asked with an agitated tone.

"Frankly, no. Of course, this is only the second day and these things do take time. I should tell you again that I'm not the police or the FBI. If you think her disappearance comes within their bailiwick, they're the people you should be talking to. Not me."

"I don't think it does. I'm sorry to be impatient, but everything is pressing down on me right now. I just wish to hell something would go right for a change." Suddenly he sounded old and crotchety. I began to feel sorry for him.

"Look, when you last saw her, did she seem upset at all?"

He studied the ice in his glass for some moments before he

replied. "Not really. Of course, she'd broken up with Jones."

"Did she tell you why?"

He shook his head. "That was her business. To be realistic about it, it was probably for the best. This still isn't the ideal country for that sort of thing. Maybe someday, but not now. Anyway, she just said they'd stopped seeing each other. That was at midterm, and I guess they didn't start up again."

I considered telling him the truth. But as I took account of his nervousness, I decided it would be better to hold off. Virginia might turn up any time, and as everyone liked to say, it was her business.

"I really wanted to see you now, because I'm going to New York today. I'll probably be back here early next week. But if you have to reach me, call my secretary." He gave me a card with his long-distance number inscribed on it.

"The thing is, I'm really in a bind now. All of the local boys are pretty much divided in their loyalties, and I've got to work fast and use some fancy footwork to stay on top of things." He paused to unwrap and light a long, narrow cigar.

"How do your chances look?" I asked.

"Oh, I think we'll pull it off, but it's going to mean a lot of work. These boys are playing dirty."

"Could Virginia be involved in any way?"

He gave me an angry look and shifted around in his seat. "I don't see how. Good God, she's certainly not disloyal!"

"I didn't say she was. But if they're playing rough, is there a possibility of kidnapping? That seems only a reasonable question."

"No, they aren't that crazy. Anyhow, we would have heard something by now, wouldn't we?" There was a note of hesitancy in the question.

"Probably," I replied. "But your opposition may still be

holding it out as a surprise. Still, I think you're right. A snatch wouldn't make much sense from their point of view."

He went to the bar and got fresh drinks for us. When he returned to the table he seemed a little less tense.

"How about her general attitude when she was home? Did you notice any change in how she thought about things?"

"Honestly, we haven't talked too much about ideas lately. We used to, a little, before she went to college. But then when she went South she became even more withdrawn. She always was a sort of introverted girl. Not that there's anything wrong in that," he added hastily.

"Did she say anything about civil rights and her ideas?" I questioned.

"Well, to be honest, I was awfully busy when she was home, and I didn't see too much of her. Irma and I had to be out a lot and then we had to go to Washington for several days just before she went back."

"Did she feel neglected?"

"Don't get me wrong. Ginny isn't one of those whining kids who complain that nobody wants them. Hell, she's been used to this sort of thing all her life. No, she didn't feel neglected." He paused and looked at me angrily across the table.

"There's no need to be offended. I'm just trying to cover everything. Remember, you know your daughter and I don't, so I have to ask to find out."

"I'm sorry. I didn't intend to be rude," he said. He leaned back in the chair.

"Now, what about Virginia's real mother?" I asked.

"Her mother, good lord!" he blurted. His astonishment at my question appeared real.

"Yes, I've heard she was talking about her before she disappeared."

with the flowers extended in front of me. She assured me of the presence of love in all places.

After a few accelerated paces I lost my loving companion. The walk was dotted here and there by neutrally dressed students coming and going with briefcases and arms filled with books. I wondered what these neutralists found to do with themselves.

I came to the large square that dominated the front of the Union. Here, some five or six card tables stood, each with its own cluster of students about it. The one I came closest to on my way in bore the sign: ASSOCIATION FOR THE DESTRUCTION OF CAPITALISM. Two bearded youths in blue work shirts and the inevitable blue jeans were selling paperback copies of *The Wretched of the Earth* by Frantz Fanon. The table next to theirs was for the Union of Democratic Socialists, and here two young men who were dressed in goatees and neat dark jackets but without ties were selling their own pile of paperbacks. I could distinguish books by Michael Harrington and Irving Howe. The crowd here was much smaller.

There was a strangely festive air about the place. Inside the main lobby of the Union were the sounds of a jukebox in a corner playing a song about a man who "blew his mind" in an automobile. Students milled about another group of card tables, including one for enlistment in the Marine Corps. A rather bewildered-looking staff sergeant with a closely cropped crew cut was handing out informational material to twins of the ROTC group I had encountered earlier.

I went to the main lounge, where I had arranged to meet Ellen. She hadn't arrived yet, so I took an easy chair near the entrance. The room was filled with a polyglot assortment of students and a few older types whom I took to be faculty members. One of these was discussing Samuel Beckett and Harold Pinter with a frightened-looking girl who looked about seventeen. They were sitting on a couch adjacent to my chair.

The man was leaning back against the armrest with his back to me. From behind he looked like a large brooding owl about to pounce on his listener. I could hear him telling her about "the existential vacuity at the center of the Beckett-Pinter universe." Her eyes never left his face and she occasionally nodded her head from side to side in bemused agreement.

I was becoming fascinated with the whole thing too when I felt a tap on my shoulder. "Hi, detective!" a feminine voice said.

Ellen Harris was standing at the side of my chair. She was dressed in a dark-blue simple suit and her auburn hair gleamed in the cold fluorescent light of the room. I noted again that she was a very good-looking girl.

"I see you're listening to Joe Randall," she said in a low tone as I stood up.

"Who's he?" I questioned. "He sounds impressive."

We strolled into the main lobby, and she put her arm through mine. "Why, he's one of our superstars. He holds the Brooks Adams Chair of Humanities for the year. Have you ever read *The Destruction of the Eagle?*"

I shook my head to indicate my ignorance of the book.

"Well, it's one of the academic best sellers. It's a study of politics and literature in turn-of-the-century America. So he's one of the biggest attractions in the graduate faculty. By the way, where would you like to eat?" She changed the subject with a soft smile.

"You know the places around here. So you tell me." We had reached the door and we stood and watched as students began to pack up their tables and equipment for the evening.

"I'd like to take you to a show here later, so how about Martin's, just across the campus?" This was a small, moderately expensive steak house that served both the university people and the nearby suburbs.

"OK with me," I said. "If we go there we might as well walk and I can avoid the parking lot crowd."

She laughed with a toss of the head. "Let's go," she said and took me by my right hand to lead me through the campus. I didn't see any more pickets of any persuasion, but the twilight would not encourage the reading of placards.

It was about six-thirty when we got to Martin's. The air-conditioning gave me a shock at first with its chill. Most of the dining room and bar crowd was made up of neat indistinguishable adults of thirty or over. Their conversation filled the room with a restrained chatter.

Ellen took most of the initiative over the dinner. She questioned me about my work and my friends. With some maneuvering I seized control through the end of the main course, and she told me of her early life in southern California and her family. Only when I asked her again about her husband did reticence overshadow the general friendliness.

"I just don't want to talk about that part of my life anymore," she said, and her lips tightened.

"Sorry," I replied. "Anyway, maybe you can fill me in with some background."

She sighed. "What kind of background?"

"Well, for example, people like those kids who chased me with flowers this afternoon. Is Virginia like that?"

"No, no," she laughed. "You see, the group you ran into were hippies. They're like my husband and I used to be. The thing for them is peace, love, drugs and a little anarchy." Her voice took on the dryness of a mildly bored lecturer who was going over worn material one time too many.

"You see, Virginia's thing is politics. She'd started out to change the government of things. Of course, her kind of person is sympathetic to the hippies, but they think basically that they're running away from life instead of really trying to change it."

"I see," I said. I wasn't at all sure I did.

"What you've got to remember is this generation isn't like any other. These kids aren't indulging themselves in panty raids. What they want is to change the entire system in one way or another." She stopped and folded her napkin by the side of her coffee cup.

"So Virginia's game is to work with Jones and his friends?"

"At one time, yes. But since I've known her, she's lost a lot of that faith." She picked up her handbag from the floor and handed me a leaflet that she took from it.

"If you go to this show with me tonight, you'll see what I mean."

The mimeographed sheet, from the Speech and Drama Department of the university, announced the presentation of a Radical/Activist Happening to be followed by a Hippie Love-in at nine o'clock. Tickets were free and were to be acquired at the Student Union.

"I've got the tickets," Ellen said. "A bunch of the campus radicals and the hippies got together to do this. They've divided the show into two parts. The first half will have antiwar skits and attacks generally on the Establishment. Then the hippies will come on and show us how to find peace and tranquillity through acid." Her mouth turned up nastily at the last phrase.

"How much drug use is there around here, by the way?" I asked.

"Oh, less than you'd think from all the talk about it, and then it's more pot than acid. But there is some acid."

"How about the police? Do they check much?"

"They sure do." She laughed. "There are a few of the older students who are definitely suspected of working for them. Every time they bust a pot party, there's a lot of suspicion but no proof."

"It's been a long time since I went to college. It seems to have changed a lot."

"You're just in that over-thirty class of people we're not supposed to trust," she said with a harsh laugh.

"Does Virginia trust her father? He's sort of an old-timer too."

"She trusts him as having good intentions at least," she replied.

"Does she have much to do at all with the hippies?"

"You mean does she use drugs. No, I'm sure of that. She doesn't dislike the hippies. They're just different, as she sees it."

"How do you see it?"

"I think it's a lot of simple-minded nonsense." She picked up her purse and headed for the ladies' room. I settled with the waiter and while I waited for her, reflected on my advanced age, which left me out of so many things.

We walked back across the campus to the Drama Building, which was only a short distance from the Student Union. The evening had grown cooler and Ellen walked close by my side, leaning against me from time to time with a light shiver.

The Drama Building was a one-story windowless stone structure with a concrete walk circling it that connected with other paths leading around the campus. Light shone through the front entrance, which stood with both doors open. Several groups of people were standing outside, as others made their way in. It was eight-thirty when we entered.

The main auditorium was directly off the foyer, and I could see corridors leading back to what I took were class-rooms. People crowded in groups, chatting and smoking in the foyer. They appeared to form a cross section of the school. There were older conservatively dressed types I took to be faculty and administrative staff. They were augmented by an assortment of students that seemed heavily weighted by beards, blue jeans and psychedelic dresses.

As we moved in the direction of the auditorium entrance, a small woman with glasses on a chain and black hair swept back in a bun took Ellen's arm and led her into a group that included Paul Howard, Joe Randall, and an older woman with bluish-gray hair and a yellow-and-pink art nouveau dress. The older woman was gesticulating with a cigarette in a short ivory holder. I followed Ellen. She introduced the black-haired woman as Sibyl Howard and the other as Violet Finch, the director of the evening's production. Howard acknowledged my presence with a curt nod and Randall pressed my hand limply.

"Why, Ellen, I didn't know you'd be here tonight," Sibyl Howard said. "If I had, I'd have asked you to join us for dinner. Anyway, you've got to come back to the house after. We're having a few people in."

The other three had gone back to their conversation. When he heard the invitation Paul Howard glanced at me. "It will be the first time we've ever had a detective in our house. Sibyl's lost her *Columbia Encyclopedia.* Maybe you can find it for her."

"Anything for a fee," I replied.

He let the exchange drop and the conversation was taken

over by Violet Finch, who seemed to think the student body should take over the school administration. She was seconded by the Howards and, with some reservations about rank and tenure, by Randall. I had nothing to contribute, so Ellen took me by the arm and led me to the auditorium. She assured the Howards we'd stop by their party if we could.

"Would you mind going?" she asked as we took our seats in the middle section. "You might find it interesting."

"Why not?" I replied. "Nothing human is alien to a detective."

6

IT WAS a few minutes after nine by my watch when the lights in the hall went out. This was followed by a series of shrieks from backstage as the lights came up on a bare stage. A group of young men in black pajamas and sandals, with their hands handcuffed behind them, were paraded onto the stage. They were followed by a sneering Uncle Sam, whose costume had been splattered with catsup to simulate blood. In his right hand he held a riding crop with which he mimed blows at the prisoners; his left hand was clenched around a toy bomb and he raised this at the audience threateningly.

When the prisoners arrived in the center of the stage, two more youths entered in Army fatigue clothes. They beat at the prisoners with wooden rifles, but the prisoners remained standing with dignified looks. Finally Uncle Sam sneered at the audience and turned back to the soldiers. At his order they raised their rifles and mimicked shooting. The prisoners crumpled to the floor slowly but with dignity.

Then the main curtain fell, and a figure came from the wings to stage center. He too was dressed in black pajamas and he held a placard which announced that blood donations for the Vietcong and bombed-out citizens of North Vietnam would be accepted the next day in room 203 of the Union. Ellen nudged me and said, "See, what price patriotism."

Before I could make any answer, the curtain rose and a blast of martial music came from the wings. I recognized the tune as the "Horst Wessel Song." Onstage a group of males and females sat at a long table, dressed in academic caps and gowns. After a period of sneering at the audience, they stood and began to curse the students and the student assembly. Their strident cries to massacre students by cutting out their brains were interrupted by a group of blue-jeaned boys who cried, "Screw President MacPherson!" and "All power to the students!" They produced rubber daggers and stabbed the faculty actors. Finally the leader of the students turned to the audience and said how sorry he was to disturb them.

Several other skits of the same type followed. In one, a trench-coated figure with a sign marked "CIA" dangling around his neck subverted a lanky boy dressed in sweater and slacks and a sign showing him to be Oswald. Another had green-bereted soldiers miming the decapitation of more prisoners. It was all climaxed by the showing of North Vietnamese films on the bombing of Hanoi.

When the lights came up for the intermission, Ellen was smiling at me. "What did you think of that?" she queried.

"They made their point. But maybe they overkilled the audience," I replied.

We moved out into the lobby and found the Howards and their guests already there in full conversational flight.

"My husband tells me you're a detective," Sibyl Howard said.

I nodded. There wasn't much else to say.

"How do you like your exposure to more open ways of

thought?" She smiled and seemed to expect me to collapse and writhe on the floor in embarrassment. I ignored the jab and listened to Violet Finch describe how she had trained and rehearsed the mime group.

"I just let them have their heads ideologically, you know. But I made them watch Keaton and Chaplin films for the past week." She had the air of a proud housemother whose group has just won the basketball trophy.

"You've done a really great job, Violet," Sibyl Howard said and was joined by a chorus of agreement from the others. "To think that in just three weeks you've been able to get this sort of result!"

The warning buzzer sounded and we made our way to our seats. Ellen was still smiling at me. "Do you think you can take the rest of it?" she queried.

"I'm learning a lot," I said. "I really have to thank you for the chance."

She laughed and took my hand as we went down the aisle. The Howards were behind us and I noticed Sibyl Howard frown at this gesture of Ellen's.

We had barely taken our seats when the clangorous sound of electric guitars came from behind the stage curtain. The melody that emerged was plaintive and twisted around and about a sharp, insistent drumbeat. A youth strode out from the wings; he was tall and gangling, with long bangs and sideburns. He was dressed in the uniform of a Confederate officer complete with sword.

"The Love-in begins," he intoned. "Now the strains of the Ad-Hoc Quartet." He returned backstage as the curtain rose to disclose three boys with electric guitars and another on drums and two girls on recorders. Their costumes were a mixture of what appeared to be cast-off sweatshirts and dirty pants. However, one of the guitarists was clad in full tails, top hat and green bowtie.

They began to chant songs about the need for love and the difficulty of achieving it. Their final number was a curse upon their parents for being alienated, depersonalized and hypocritical. There was also some criticism because the parents lived in the suburbs.

In all, five groups played that evening. They had names like The Lumpenproletariat and The Swan and The Thankful Cookie. There was little difference among the songs; they all moved from complaint to love. For costumes the performers ran a gamut from togas and vine leaves to *Wehrmacht* uniforms complete with helmets and swastikas.

The last group to play was named The Final Solution and they were the ones dressed in the German uniforms. They began by hurling tulips at the audience. The four boys who made up the group were bearded and had beads of various colors about their necks.

Their first number described an air raid murdering lovers and their second detailed the beauties of an LSD trip. But the third brought the evening to a close as they sang of the need to kill, kill with love those who hurt love. At the end, the drummer stood in front of his kit and kicked it to pieces as the other members intoned their hatred of haters.

The music continued to beat an insistent pattern in my head as we walked across the campus to the parking lot. Ellen laughed again and asked, "How did you like the music?"

"Very interesting," I said. "But it must be expensive to buy a new drum every time that group plays."

"Oh, they don't usually go that far. But tonight was sponsored by the Allison Foundation, so they picked up the tab for everything. It's part of their program to foster campus rebellion in the arts. By the way, my husband used to play lead guitar in a group like that," she concluded.

"What did you do while he played?" I asked.

"Oh, I used to sing. We called ourselves The Mushrooms, after the hallucinating mushrooms. Wrote our own stuff and all that."

"Looking at you now, I can't imagine you in those circumstances. You look like a model middle-class girl."

"Right now I'm really nothing," she answered. "You see, I don't really know where I belong. I'm not a hippie anymore and I'm not radical. I just go through motions, I guess." She sounded as though she had given a lot of thought to her not belonging.

By the time we reached the car, a light breeze had come up and brought with it some cooling drops of rain. When I got into my side, she leaned over and kissed me. I let the kiss take its course and then started the motor.

"Do you think Virginia shared your feelings before she left?" I asked as soon as we got clear of the lot and she had given me directions to the Howards'.

"You bastard!" She laughed. "Can't you ever stop working and give a girl a break?"

"I'm always working. It helps me restrain my libido and keeps me from attacking pretty girls who are too young for me."

The Howards lived in one of the newer upper-class suburbs. Its houses were custom designed so that no two were alike. For owners, the realtors had deliberately sought the higher-income groups. The Howards' home was situated behind a circle that ended the street. The circle was large and covered with grass, trees and a few well-spaced benches. In effect it was a small park. Behind it the Howards' house sat spaciously but neatly, with a carefully trimmed lawn and a lighted coach lamp; the house itself was of two-story Georgian design, painted a light gray.

Several guests had preceded us and I had to hunt awhile to find a parking spot, a short walk from the house.

As we strolled toward the lamp, Ellen said, "I'm not sure who the rest of the guests are. But you'll probably meet some people who knew Virginia."

"What about CeeJay?" I asked. I had told her about my encounters with him.

"No, he doesn't have much to do with these people socially. They may have radical ideas, but they are white."

The front door to the house stood slightly ajar, so we walked into the hall and stepped through the inner door to the main part of the house. We entered a well-appointed living room with neat oak furniture and eighteenth-century prints on the walls. This room extended halfway through the house, with a stairway on the side and a passage through to the kitchen. Immediately off the living area was a dining room with French doors, which gave onto a terrace. A long, thick dining-room table was piled with hors d'oeuvres and there was a small bar to the side from which guests were making their own drinks. The doors to the terrace were open and people were standing with their drinks under the terrace awning in spite of the breeze and the sprinkling of rain.

Sibyl Howard saw us as we came in and broke away from a group of young men, some of whom I had seen in the mime performance earlier.

"I'm glad you decided to come, Ellen. You, too, Mr. Foley," she added as an afterthought. "Thank God, today was the last day of classes and we can let off some steam tonight."

Sibyl Howard took me by the arm and led me to the side of the room, where there was a gap between two groups of middle-aged academic-appearing types. As she did so, Ellen moved away and began to talk with Paul Howard, who was mixing a martini at the bar.

"Mr. Foley, just a word. I'm sorry if we seemed a little unfriendly earlier," Sibyl Howard said with what seemed to be an ingratiating smile. "You see, we're rather insular actually, and we don't see many people who aren't connected with academic life."

"That's OK," I said. "I'm not thin-skinned enough to let something like that bother me."

"And I want you to know that if there's anything my husband and I can do to help you find Virginia, we're at your service."

"Thanks. If you have some time tomorrow, I'd like to talk with you. This doesn't seem like the right place or time," I answered.

"You're right. Now, I'll be in my office in Edmonds Hall about four tomorrow. Why don't you come. In the meantime, help yourself to the drinks and food."

She touched my sleeve lightly and walked across the room to turn on the stereo against the far wall. The soft throb of Ravi Shankar's music began to fill the room. Then she moved off to where Joe Randall, Violet Finch and a tall, bearded man with curly black hair and an English tweed suit stood talking.

I remained isolated for a few moments and then I responded to a nod from Ellen; I joined her and Paul Howard at the bar.

"I'm sorry I've been so salty, Foley," he said as a greeting. "How about a drink to show there are no hard feelings?" His heartiness seemed somewhat forced.

I said I'd take a bourbon on the rocks and assured him I wasn't holding any grudges.

"Ellen tells me you found the show interesting," he went on.

"It was a little frantic, I thought."

"Oh, sure, but you've got to realize these boys and girls are just feeling their commitment. They're alive with it, and life is often frantic." He seemed unable to speak without lecturing.

"Too much life can kill too, Paul," Ellen interrupted.

"Ellen, Ellen, wait," Howard said with a quick downward motion of his left hand. "You've had a bad break, I know. But when you're living on the frontiers of human experience, accidents happen. Is it better to go through life as a suburban zombi, a plaything of fat creeps on Madison Avenue? What do you think, Foley?" He turned to me with an intense look.

"I can't say. I'm not sure I understand what you're getting at."

"What I'm getting at! Why, man, look at our neighbors, smug and content with the pap that pours out of their boob tubes. They don't live, they don't have personalities. They're nothing." He was so engrossed in his own words that he started when Violet Finch tapped him on the arm.

"Can I intrude for a drink?" she asked with a genteel smile.

"Violet, you're the heroine of the evening. Anything you want," he said and poured her a Manhattan from a pitcher without asking her for her choice.

"You know, Foley, this is one hell of a woman," he said and took her by the arm to draw her into our circle. "Violet is really helping American theater come alive again. We're lucky to have her here."

I nodded in meaningless agreement.

"She used to run The Turned-on House in the Village. Sibyl

75

and I saw our first real Happening there. Lord, I still remember having to walk into the theater with the actors grabbing and pummeling us. But it was a real communal experience."

"We tried, Paul," Violet said. "But the fuzz were against us. Snatched away that license, just because poor dear John was selling acid. Shut out, that's what happened, and after so much work." Her smile had changed to an agitated frown.

She turned to me and said, "I'm afraid this must sound very foolish to you, Mr. Foley, but after twenty-five years in the theater to finally have something of your own, and then they just snatch it away from you." She was very effective, and there was even a glint of tears in her eyes as she spoke to me.

"Anyway, Violet, you've come to a place now where you can be appreciated," Howard interjected. "It was probably for the best, if you look at it properly. Here you have more and even better opportunities for real theater. So the state pays the bill. Look at what Brecht got out of German bureaucrats!"

"Brecht." She sneered the name as if someone had referred to an old enemy. "So overrated these days, Paul. No spontaneity there. Really, he's as old-fashioned as the Moscow Theater."

"Just a comparison, Violet, no offense," Howard said with a laugh and a shrug of his shoulders.

I edged forward to the bar and made another highball for myself. At Ellen's nod I poured her another martini from the pitcher. We stood off a little ways to ourselves and sampled some shrimp hors d'oeuvres from the table. The Beatles had taken over from Ravi Shankar and their voices resounded in the air.

"Sometimes I think I should have just gone to a business school and become a secretary," Ellen said.

Before I could reply we were joined by Joe Randall, who had

obviously either a low tolerance for alcohol or had been at it too much. He was accompanied by the bearded man in the tweed suit whom I had noticed earlier.

"Mrs. Harris, good to see you," he said. His voice was clear but his phrasing and intonation revealed his condition. "This is Dr. Wilson. I don't think you've met."

He introduced us to the other man, who silently acknowledged the meeting by a curt nod of the head. I followed his lead and did not extend my hand.

Randall put his arms around Wilson and Ellen and drew them into a half circle facing me. "Do you know this bird's private fuzz?" he asked the bearded man.

Wilson didn't answer; he only glanced at me with curiosity.

"Yeah, he's trying to find out what happened to the McReedy broad," Randall went on. "He's probably going to report us all as subversives and acid heads to our friends in the Police Department. That right, fuzz?"

Before he could say anything more, Ellen worked herself loose from his arm about her waist. She took his elbow and led him away on the pretext that she wanted another drink. As she went, she winked at me and turned down the corners of her mouth in a mock grimace.

I was left alone with Wilson. After a few moments of desultory conversation I learned that he was a colleague of Howard's in the Philosophy Department and that he specialized in mathematical logic.

"I'm afraid I can't be of any help to you about Miss McReedy," he said suddenly. "She took my elementary course a year or so ago. But I only knew her slightly."

"How was she as a student?" I asked.

"Well, Paul tells me she used to be first-rate, although her work has fallen off lately, he claims. All I can say is she'd never make it as a logician. Very fine girl, though. I respect her civil rights work. Took a lot of courage to do what she did. I know I wouldn't have that much nerve."

"How about CeeJay Jones? Is he one of your students?"

Morris looked at me suspiciously and said, "I've never had Mr. Jones in my class." He turned quickly and walked away to join Ellen and Randall, with another group near the stereo. Ellen smiled at me across the room.

I drifted around the guests for a while like the Ancient Mariner searching for someone to tell his tale to. But the faces I encountered were unfamiliar and the thought of joining Randall and Wilson again was unappealing. After another drink I stood outside on the terrace and breathed the fresh air. The rain had stopped and there was still a slight chill in the air. But it was not unpleasant and a full moon had emerged from the clouds and was casting a soft light over the lawn. The yard was large and extended for some distance into the shadows, where the mass of a house on the next street lowered over the shrubbery. The terrace was bare of people and I stood for a while under the lights. Then I walked out into the yard and sat on a bench under a maple tree at the side of the house.

I had been there only a minute or two when four boys from the mime troupe came out of the doors and sat on wicker chairs that were spaced in a circle on the terrace. They had brown paper cigarettes in their hands and as soon as they were seated they set fire to them. I was close enough to the group to catch the acrid aroma of marihuana. It was no business of mine, so I remained seated and watched them become lethargic and relaxed.

Then Paul Howard stepped outside and shut the terrace doors quickly. "You God-damned fools," he snarled. "Don't you have more brains than to smoke pot here? There's a private cop in the house, and maybe even a spy from the fuzz. Get rid of it now."

They put the cigarettes out on the concrete floor of the terrace in such a way that they were able to preserve the stubs, which they placed in their pockets. Then they followed Howard inside. I was sufficiently in the shadows to pass unobserved. I continued to sit for a while and then made my way back inside.

The crowd of guests had increased somewhat, with even more tousled, shaggy students in evidence. I couldn't see the Howards anywhere, but Ellen was standing alone by the bar.

"Nice to see you again," she said when I came up to her. "I thought you'd gone and left me to cope with Randall. I just called him an old goat when he asked me to spend the night with him."

"Let's go," I said.

"I'm glad you're taking the hint," she replied.

We didn't bother searching for the Howards. The sight of Randall staggering toward us provided sufficient impetus to put us on our way.

We made it out of the door before Randall could catch up with us. As we stepped onto the sidewalk I saw Violet Finch climbing into a blue Volkswagen. She gunned the motor fast, stalled and started it again before she got away. Her driving pattern was a little erratic at first as she swerved around in the road, but she finally seemed to take control in a definite direction toward the city.

"Looks as though Violet may have had a drop too much," I said.

"She's not the only one. God, Randall is such a slob when he starts to drink. But even Sibyl had a few too many. Before you got me out, I heard her call Paul a coward and a back-slider in the kitchen. Maybe I should blackmail him. You know, 'Fearless professor's wife thinks him cowardly.'" She laughed with a malicious tone.

"So everyone has fights," I said.

"Not the Howards. They're too civilized," she countered. "Anyway, I hope your time wasn't wasted." The last was said with feminine sarcasm.

We reached my car, and I helped Ellen inside. "Well, I didn't find out anything about Virginia, but it was helpful to see the kind of milieu she moved in," I said as I got behind the wheel.

"'Milieu.' My lord, that's fancy! Now how about driving me to my place or your place and having a drink?"

I agreed to taking her home, and she gave me an address on one of the better midtown residential streets. "You see, I use the blood money from my husband's parents for the rent," she explained. "The rest comes from my assistantship and the typing I do on the side."

As we drove I told her about the scene I had observed between Howard and the students.

"I'm not surprised. Most of those kids smoke pot at least. And, as I told you, they're damned nervous about the police."

"How about Howard?"

"He's not a user. But he's very sympathetic."

"He seems very worried about the police."

"Sure he is. You know the cops in this city resent the bearded professors and everything they stand for. Last month they pulled a raid on some kids in their apartment. It's true they're users, but at the time the place was completely clean." She leaned her head in my direction to emphasize the last point.

"Let me guess," I said. "They busted in and dropped a package of marihuana on the table. One of the guys looks surprised to see what they've found. Then everyone's booked. Am I right?" I asked.

"I see you know what happened," she replied.

"No, but I was once a cop. I do know how the guys in that branch do things. I don't approve, in case you wondered."

"I don't care whether you do or not. I don't even care myself. My place is the first one on the right."

She lived in an old but well-kept apartment house some five stories high. It was close to two o'clock when we found a parking space.

"Come up for a drink or something," she said with a smile.

She took my arm tightly with her hand and led me up the sidewalk. I could feel her leaning into my side as we walked. I began to debate with myself internally about the pros and cons of the situation.

She fumbled in her purse for a moment to find the key to the outer door. When she located it and opened the door, she caught me in her arms as I followed her inside. She kissed me with force, and I let myself return it. We were silent on the way up in the self-service elevator.

Her apartment was on the fourth floor. It had a small living area with comfortable maple chairs and a sofa. There was a portable TV on a stand, and a small stereo set was placed on a bookcase against the wall. A kitchenette opened off the room and there was a closed door opposite, which led, I presumed, to the bedroom. Books and records were laid askew in the bookcase and a typewriter surrounded by piles of typed sheets rested on a desk at the side of the room.

"Now that you're here safely, I'm going," I said with a certain feeling of pride at my strength of character.

"Why?" she asked.

"For too many reasons to go into," I answered. "Let's just say I think you've had too many troubles recently to be objective about things right now."

"When can I see you?"

"I'll call you," I said as I opened the door to let myself out.

On my way down in the elevator I forced myself to be reasonable and recognize that I had taken the sane and sensible course of action. It wasn't much comfort, but then an affair with a distraught girl whose husband was in an asylum wouldn't be too comfortable either. By the time I reached my own apartment, my stoicism was easier to live with.

7

↶ IT WAS after three by the time I got back to my apartment. I was tired enough to want to think only of a good night's sleep and to forget about missing girls and college students. However, as soon as I turned on the lights, I saw I had a cleaning-up job to do. The cushions of the chairs were upside down on the floor, and books and papers were scattered about the living room. Mr. O'Connor and his employers obviously would not be pushed around with impunity.

I made myself some coffee and had two cups to get enough energy for the job. After a half hour's work, I had the majority of the things in their places. Finally I undressed and readied myself for what I thought was a well-earned rest.

But as I was about to turn out the lights, my telephone gave a harsh cry. When I picked up the receiver, the speaker identified herself as a Western Union operator. She read me a message from Irma McReedy: Mrs. McReedy wished me to meet her at my office at noon.

I arrived at my office a little before noon. The mess that met me announced another visit from my official acquaintances.

With muttered oaths I set myself to my second clean-up job. I had just finished throwing the papers back in my desk drawers and filing cabinet when the outer door was opened.

The woman was tall and in her late forties. She had dark hair with just touches of gray scattered through it. Her appearance was attractive and her face was pleasant and good-natured.

"Hello, I'm Irma McReedy," she said as she stood at the threshold. I acknowledged the introduction and sat her in the client's chair. She crossed her legs and folded her hands in her lap, on her purse. There was no appearance of nervousness or tension in her bearing.

"My husband got back last night. After I'd met him and we'd talked, I had to see you and set you straight," she said.

"Set me straight? I'm not sure I follow," I replied.

"Well, it's unfair to you and to us as your clients if you don't know the whole story. But you see, my husband's so upset about the coming election and Ginny's vanishing and all. So he's not really using his head." The way she let it all pour out belied the surface calmness of her manner.

"Just a minute," I said. "Suppose we start at the beginning. What is the whole story that I don't know? You're right, it's pretty hard to do this sort of job unless you know what it is you're doing."

"The thing is, my husband just didn't tell you all. We had a telephone call from Ginny the same day we received her letter. That's what you didn't know."

"OK," I said. "You'd better let me have the full story."

"We were getting ready to go off on another vote-hunting trip when Virginia's letter came," she said, speaking slowly and clearly. "Actually we weren't too disturbed by the letter. Virginia's always been treated sensibly."

"So I've heard before. But she doesn't seem to be acting too sensibly now." I was sorry I'd snapped when I saw the shadow of dismay that crossed her face.

"I know. Anyway, a couple of hours after the letter came, she phoned us long distance from here. The call was collect," she added as an afterthought.

"What was the matter?" I asked.

"Even now we don't know. She was incoherent. All she did was cry and insist that we come here at once. She started to talk about her mother, Rita." She paused for a moment to re-establish her calmness.

"Who took the call?" I asked. "You or your husband?"

"I did," she replied.

"Just exactly what did she say?"

"It's hard to be clear about it," she said in a perplexed tone. "She was crying, and she wanted us to come here. She said she'd get in touch with us at the Manor Hotel, where we usually stay."

"Where was she calling from?"

"I don't know, and I was so surprised I didn't think to ask. That was stupid of me."

"It's not always easy to think of everything under pressure," I said. "But what did she say about her mother?"

She was silent for several moments, and I could see that the general topic was painful to her. "Just that she'd seen her mother and she had to see us. Then she cried some more and said that we'd have to make everything up to her."

"What did she mean by that?" I asked.

"I have no idea. I tried to talk sense to her, but she kept sobbing and crying. It was just impossible to get anything definite from her."

"So what happened?"

"We took a plane and got here that night."

"What did she say when you saw her?"

"That's just it. We never saw her. She never showed up at the hotel."

"What did you do then?" I queried.

"We waited through the next day, and then we checked with her landlady and Paul Howard. But no one had any idea where she was." She was obviously upset now, and taking a lace handkerchief from her purse, she twisted and knotted it between her fingers.

"So when you heard nothing from her, you just went about your business, is that it?" I tried to keep from sounding too sarcastic.

"I know it sounds heartless. But what could we do? There wasn't any point in sitting around doing nothing."

"You could have called the police," I countered.

"Yes, but unfortunately we aren't ordinary people, and a lot of important things hinge on my husband's winning the election." It was a bare statement, not a plea for mercy or pity. "We waited through the next day and the night. After that we had to leave," she went on.

"All right, you both had your reasons for what you did. It's none of my affair whether you were justified or not. But why did you wait so long to hire me?"

She looked at me. "We didn't know what to do. Really, we're completely bewildered about the whole affair," she went on.

"OK, but at least I could have been told about her mother. How in hell can I work in the dark?"

"Of course you're entirely right. My husband just couldn't believe Rita was really involved in this in any way. Frankly, he's ashamed of what happened, with her abandoning him and all."

She stopped for a moment and then continued. "And to be honest, an old scandal revived wouldn't help him very much right now."

"What do you think about her mother's supposed reappearance?"

"I don't understand it at all. My husband told her all there was to know about him and Rita. It's just incredible to think of her coming around now after so many years. Why, Virginia wouldn't even remember her! She never knew her."

"People do have changes of heart," I said. "Maybe she became remorseful after all those years and decided it was time she found her daughter."

"Virginia doesn't need to have anything made up to her," she answered, with hostility evident in her voice.

"It's only fair to tell you that I haven't got anywhere," I said to temper her anger. "The thing is, I've got the impression Virginia was going through some sort of crisis."

"What do you mean?"

I related what I learned from my questioning of the previous days, but I left out the marriage.

She thought in silence for a few minutes and then said, "You may be right. Actually the Southern experience was pretty traumatic for her, and I know she's been worried about her father's election."

"Well, leaving aside this mother issue, do you think she was upset enough to have a breakdown and wander away?" I asked.

"I don't think so. But let me be frank with you: this has been a hectic year and we haven't had as much to do with Virginia as we ordinarily would."

"I can understand. But check me if I'm right. I get the impression of a sensitive, quiet but basically stable person."

"You're right," she said. "I just can't understand what's going on now."

"I'm still trying to find out," I said.

She smiled for the first time, and I could see she was a person who held herself with dignity and humor.

"Mr. Foley, I'm going to stay on here until we do find out what has happened. I'll be at the hotel. Please keep me posted."

After she left I sat for a while and watched the light-gray clouds settle over the skyline as the breeze pushed them in from the lake. They were blotting out the sun and making the day dull. Finally I stirred myself from lethargy and went down to a small bar around the corner. A beer and a roast beef sandwich revived my stomach but failed to do much for my brain.

At one o'clock I went back to my desk and called Al Morgan at the Hall of Justice. Al is a special detective with the Department's Office of Investigation. That's a portentous name for the unit that moves in on any particularly important case of whatever type, from murder to vice. He said he'd see me in his office in a half hour.

I made my way through the crowds of afternoon shoppers, who were not to be deterred by the threatening clouds. But by the time I cut across to the side street where the Hall was located, I had only a few staggering stumblebums as companions.

Morgan is about my age, and we had joined the force together. He's a short, squat man with a considerable paunch. His curly black hair lords it over a round Irish face, from which a black cigar usually juts out. On the whole he resembles a more shady than average used-car dealer. But he's tough and honest. He occupies a small dark cubicle in the back of the Hall.

When I stepped into his office I found him with his feet on the edge of the desk, going through a folder of mug shots.

"Hello, John. Good to see you, for Christ's sake," he said and stood up to extend his hand. "How's things going in private work? You know, sometimes I'm almost inclined to join you."

"Glad to have you, Al," I said as I shook his hand. I took a seat in the chair at the side of his desk and lit a cigarette to fight against the fumes of his cigar, which smoldered in an ashtray.

"What can I do for you, John?" he asked.

"How about filling me in on the narcotics situation at the university?" I asked.

He frowned and replaced his feet on the desk. "That's not my department, John. You know that. Why don't you ask O'Brien?"

"Come on, Al," I said. "That moralistic bastard and I couldn't even agree on how to shut a window!"

"OK," he answered. "Are you onto something in that line?"

"Maybe, maybe not. I have to keep the case quiet. But I wouldn't buck you guys, if it came to that."

"But it hasn't, I take it?" he asked.

I shook my head. He took his time in having a few puffs from the cigar and some more smoke joined the general haze of the office.

"Most of the stuff out there is pot, as you probably know," he went on. "Oh, there's some LSD, but not to any great extent."

"How do they get hold of it?" I asked.

"All sorts of ways. Some grow it, a lot of them bring it in from Mexico during vacation, some make connections in the ghetto." He stopped for a moment, and then went on. "There's no way, as you know, of eliminating the sources."

"How about the syndicates? Are they getting into the action at all?"

"No. For guys like that this sort of thing is strictly penny-ante. What you have here is really a sort of cult."

"A cult?"

He stubbed his cigar butt out in the ashtray and leaned back farther in the swivel chair. "Sure, that's what it is. Look, John, these students are really out to tell us we're all a bunch of hypocrites."

"I agree," I said. "But where does the cult come in?"

"It's a unity, I suppose, of attitude. That's a pompous way of saying they stick together in their ideas. Of course, as far as numbers go, they're strictly a minority. Hell, for most of the kids going to school out there, nothing suits them better than coeds, liquor and fraternities. Just like us."

"Speak for yourself," I replied.

He laughed and jabbed the air with his right forefinger to emphasize his point. "OK, so you went to an all-male school buried in the woods. But my point still holds good. To smoke pot is to say that all of us in our thirties and beyond smoke and get cancer. Or we drink and become alcoholics and kill people with drunken driving."

"You can't say they don't have a point anyway."

"Sure, we all know that. The pot is probably not particularly dangerous in itself. But it's the attitude that goes with it; that's what's so upsetting. It's an attitude of rejection of responsibility and everything that goes with it that gets people."

"So what's being done?"

"By me, not a damn thing." He turned in the chair for a moment and looked out of the window, half of which was blocked by the sight of the right wing of the building. "But O'Brien's expanding his squad and popping up all over the God-damned place on TV and in the newspapers."

"I've seen some of it."

He swung back in the chair and faced me. "Sure, it's the greatest thing that's ever come his way. And the judges!" He shook his head sadly as he paused. "Why that crazy son of a bitch Moore gave one kid five years for peddling. He was a grad student and special James Scholar."

"They're really guardians of the public morals, aren't they," I said with a laugh. "How about informers?"

"How about 'em?" he answered with a blank but knowing look.

"Just that," I retorted. "Is O'Brien using them? If so, who, and how does he recruit them?"

"Well, OK," he answered. "I don't have to tell you that nothing about this is to get out. O'Brien is a son of a bitch, but he's our son of a bitch."

I nodded to agree.

"There are a few informers. Not too many. Actually no more than four. He gets them by blackmail. Some involved in a minor scrape, shoplifting or auto trouble. He gets the arresting section to cooperate. They drop the charge or fix it on condition the guy finks on campus activities."

"Are there just students involved?" I asked.

"All but one, and he's a big one. Ever hear of Dr. Joseph Randall?"

I nodded again.

"Well, he's close to a lot of hippies. Last fall, his boy, who goes to another college out of town, hit and injured a kid while he was driving drunk. We killed the charge and the arresting officer said the Randall brat was sober and that it was an unavoidable accident. Kid ran into the street."

"Has Randall been much help?" I queried.

"According to O'Brien, he's been great. We know the name and address of nearly every user. Any time O'Brien's boys need a crackdown for some publicity, they know who to plant the stuff on or to raid when it's already there."

"Thanks a lot, Al," I said as I got up to leave. "You've been a help."

We shook hands again and he said, "Glad to help. But don't use any of it in public."

I assured him I wouldn't and left him lighting another cigar.

When I arrived at the campus I could see that the end of the semester had already taken its toll. The parking area was sparsely populated with cars, and an air of muted desolation seemed to possess the area. Only a few clusters of students were to be seen when I walked again through the crisscrossed walks that led to the various halls of learning.

Sibyl Howard's office was in the Edmonds Hall of Social Science. This was a four-story edifice, which looked as if it were constructed inside and outside of fragile blue-tinted glass. It wasn't, because dark areas of concrete cut across the glass, but their presence was obscured by the play of light from inside and outside.

I found Sibyl Howard's name in a directory next to the door. She was located on the third floor in the middle of the building. The hall was deserted save for a charwoman, who was beginning to mop down the scuffed corridor floors. I knocked on the door and Mrs. Howard's voice told me to come in.

Her office was furnished in gleaming white and orange. The desk behind which she sat seemed to be only a slab held up by toothpicks. Recessed bookshelves were packed with books and periodicals. Fluorescent lamps suspended from the ceiling by narrow posts cast an antiseptic glow over the room.

She was going through pages of a manuscript with a red pencil clenched in the fingers of her right hand. "I'm glad you could come, Mr. Foley," she said.

"Frankly, I hope you may be able to give me some kind of lead," I answered.

She looked at me squarely and smiled with what seemed meant to convey goodwill but suggested malevolence. "You know, Mr. Foley, your work must bring you into contact with all sorts of things I'm interested in." Evidently she meant to ignore the purpose of my visit.

"I don't understand," I said.

"You see, I'm working on a book that deals with the reactions of people under stress."

"That doesn't tell me much," I countered, and I didn't bother to conceal my annoyance.

"Oh, I think you do. I'm trying to graph the ways people, particularly middle-class ones, have of adjusting to the social world when they are frightened, shocked or in danger."

"What do you do—hang around street corners and wait for auto accidents?" I asked.

"In a way." She laughed. "Of course, my assistants do the actual interviewing. But I do talk with people in the emergency ward. Last winter I went out to the Coast and did some interviewing of returning combat veterans who'd been wounded."

"It sounds rather ghoulish," I said.

"Surely no more than your own business. After all, you make your living off human troubles," she replied.

"Sure, but sometimes I may do something helpful for the ones who hire me."

She glanced down at the typewritten pages that were the only objects on the white surface of the desk. "Well, my backers think highly enough of the practical possibilities of my work to pay for it and its publication. Really, I can't get over the antiquated notions laymen have of the social sciences."

"I don't have any notions one way or the other, Mrs. Howard."

She pursed her lips and put her right hand behind her head to feel the bun there. After she seemed certain it was still there, she picked up the pencil and turned it in her fingers.

"All right then, how do you think I can help you?" she asked.

"For a start, do you have any idea what could have happened to Virginia McReedy?"

"You've already asked my husband that," she said coldly.

"I know, but I thought perhaps a woman might have more ideas than a man. I mean she might have confided in you."

She laughed and displayed even white teeth. "I assure you you overestimate the extent of my friendship with the girl."

"Maybe, but I have to check everything."

She smiled tolerantly at me. "No, all I mean to say is she was actually closer to my husband. He was the one who introduced her to our circle."

"You sound as though you don't particularly like her."

"Not at all. She's a very fine person. At the present time she's perhaps a little more confused than is good for her." She looked directly at me again, and I could detect distinct animosity in her eyes.

"I don't understand," I said. "You mean because she seems to have got herself lost in some way?"

"I can't say anything about that, because I don't know anything about it. I do know she holds some very strange ideas for someone who took the chances she's supposed to have taken in the South." She snapped the last sentence out with disdain.

"Supposed to have taken?" I asked.

"Well, all right, that she did take. After all, CeeJay still swears by her even now." She stopped for a moment as if to consider her next words carefully.

"What I mean to say is that anyone who has identified with the underdog in the world struggle now going on shouldn't cast doubts on the very integrity of the struggle."

For a moment I thought I was in a lecture hall. "Just what is it she casts doubt on?"

"You wouldn't have heard of Michels, I suppose." The tone suggested that it would be a world-shaking miracle if I had.

"No, why?"

"He was a fascist," she snorted. "Some of the new imperialists here in this very department believe in him. Anyway, he held that the power in any organization sooner or later came into the hands of an oligarchy."

"So?"

"Certainly, if you try to help the wretched of the world to achieve true democracy, you can't cast doubt on the whole enterprise at the start."

"Is that what Virginia was doing?"

"Yes." Her voice was marked by reserved petulance. "Why, just before she disappeared she told me that we were all engaged in the battle for our personal aggrandizement."

I laughed. "Are you?"

"Now just a minute, Mr. Foley, I didn't ask you here to be insulted."

"Why did you ask me then?"

She rested her arms on the desktop and looked at the papers in front of her again. "Despite it all, we're fond of the girl and would like to help you."

"OK then. When did Virginia start to have these ideas?"

"I can't say. I first noticed it when I finished interviewing her."

"What were you interviewing her about?" I questioned.

"I'm using her as one of the cases in my book. Her experiences in the South are invaluable as a study in stress."

"So what did you find out?"

"Just that she was becoming a neoconservative," she replied.

"That doesn't tell me much."

"I'm afraid that's the only way I can put it. She was giving up all of her idealism for cynicism."

"Would that have made her want to vanish?" I asked.

"I can't answer that. I do know she was breaking away from her old friends."

"You mean CeeJay?"

"Him and even us."

"You mean she told you she didn't want anything more to do with you?" I queried.

"Nothing that overt. Actually we were the ones who would have had to exclude her," she said and then began to pick up the papers and place them in an attaché case that stood open at the side of the desk.

"Is it fair to think, then, that you were going to exclude her? Rather than the other way around?"

"Not at all. She was making us drop her by joining the

enemy, that's all." She shut the case with a bang and stood up. "I'm sorry to cut this short, Mr. Foley, but I must go."

I stood up and held the door open for her. "Just a moment, Mrs. Howard," I said. "Could I see your case report on Virginia?"

"Certainly not. That's private research." She strode down the hallway without waiting for me.

I went back to my car and sat for a few moments, considering the job I was doing. On the whole, I couldn't see that I was getting anywhere. There were no leads in particular, and I just seemed to be making myself enemies.

Finally I started the engine and drove out in the direction of my apartment. I considered calling Ellen to have dinner with me, but rejected the idea on the grounds that it would be better for me if she didn't.

I was just making coffee and brooding on what kind of TV dinner I should have when the telephone rang. The voice was Ellen's but it sounded constricted and tense.

"Hello, John," she said. "Please, it's important. I've got to see you here right away."

"Where's here?" I asked.

"My place," she answered. "Come over now, please. I can't say anything more on the phone."

I told her I'd be right over, and she hung up without a further word. My mood wasn't too pleasant as I turned off the coffee and gave up my idea of a restful evening. The idea of seeing Ellen had its attractions, but again, what was the point? Traffic was light at that time of the early evening, and I made it to her apartment in less than fifteen minutes.

There was no answer from the house phone as I pressed the buzzer. My only reply was the click that released the

97

lock of the door. When I arrived at her floor there was no sound from behind the door. I knocked and when the door opened I was looking into the wrong end of a Smith & Wesson .38 Chief Special.

The man behind the gun was not a cop, however. He was short and stocky, with heavy bulky shoulders. His features were mashed and squeezed together, with a bulbous red-veined nose in the center.

He motioned me into the room with a flick of the gun barrel. I saw Ellen crouched in a corner chair with her feet drawn under her. Behind her chair was a tall man with a rodent-like pockmarked face and sallow complexion.

I recognized the pair as Rick "Big Nose" Cass and Morty "Rat Face" Morton. They are two small-time muscle men who work for Simon Damma, the local syndicate boss. Cass motioned me to stand within arm's length of him and removed the gun from my shoulder holster. I missed its presence.

"I'm sorry, John," Ellen said in a frightened voice. "They made me call you. If I wouldn't, they threatened to mark me up good."

"That's OK," I said. "That's about all these hoods would know how to do. Brains they haven't got."

"Come on, smart mouth," Cass snarled. "Someone wants to see you. The broad too."

Ellen looked at me for guidance. "Do as he says," I said. "He has the gun."

They motioned me out of the door first. Ellen was kept between the two as we rode down in the elevator, and I was placed in front. We stayed like this all the way to the car, which was parked only a short distance from the front entrance. It was a new four-door gray Cadillac. I was shoved into the back with Cass, and Ellen sat in front with Morton.

As we drove she turned to look back at me and I could see the fear marked clearly in her eyes. I hoped my own wasn't showing as much.

"Try not to be nervous," I said. "These birds have just seen too many movies and too much TV. They think they've got to act like this to keep up their image." This brought no response from the pair, and it didn't seem to help Ellen much either.

Cass had kept the gun in his pocket on the way out. Once inside the car, he took it out again and held it pointed at me with his hand poised on his knee. I kept watching for an opening, but nothing presented itself on the way.

We cut through the downtown area and up to Central Avenue. The stores were mostly shut for the evening, with only an occasional restaurant showing lights and people. I felt isolated from the rest of the world.

Finally we pulled into a parking space in front of an old brownstone house that had been remodeled into a restaurant. It is called Damma's Den and it's one of the more expensive places in town. However, now the neon sign along the top of the front bay window was dark, and the curtains were drawn across the window itself. A sign, CLOSED FOR REMODELING, was tacked to the front door.

They marched us up the walk and into the dark foyer, with me in front again. Once inside, Cass prodded me in the back with the gun and pushed me into the bar.

Here the subdued wall lights on the side were on. The back section, which was the restaurant proper, was curtained off, and buckets of paint stood in front of the curtain. There were small tables with big captain's chairs set around the bar area.

Simon Damma was seated at one of the tables close to the bar. His features are full and flushed and he must tip the

99

scales at about two hundred or more. He has only a short formal record for an assault or two in his early years in Brooklyn. However, his informal record is long and detailed; but the details would never stand up in court. From time to time he's identified as a top syndicate figure, but this just makes his restaurant a bit more glamorous.

Cass pushed me into a chair facing Damma but quite a way back from him. Then he moved back to where Morton was standing by the bar with Ellen.

"Mr. Foley, I have some questions to ask you," Damma said and put his hands on the tabletop. "I want answers. Then you and the young lady are free to go on your way."

"The hell you say," I replied.

"We've never met, Mr. Foley. But I'm sure you know of me from your time on the force. I'm equally sure you're aware that I usually get my way." His voice was deep with an oddly reedy quality.

"Usually, but not always," I answered. "Look, Damma, I don't give a howl in hell for what you want. If you wanted to talk to me, then you could have come to my office. But no, you've got to try intimidation. So you send these stumblebums to terrorize me. It won't work." Actually it had worked, but that fact was nothing to bargain with.

He laughed and shook his head back and forth several times. "Please, Mr. Foley, no false bravado. Look at the facts, my dear man. You are unarmed and in the presence of two men who, regardless of what you may think of their brains, will do exactly what I tell them."

I held myself erect in the chair and tried to relax the tension in my muscles as much as possible. "Yeah, yeah, they're very frightening. OK, now that we're here, what's on your mind?"

"Where's Virginia McReedy and why has she dropped from sight?" he asked.

"You tell me," I replied.

"Mr. Foley, please don't let's have to resort to nasty methods," he said unctuously. "Your humor is poorly suited to the occasion."

"It's not funny, Damma. If you think I know, your information's lousy."

"Come on, Foley," he snapped. "You're looking for the bitch and I want to know why and what you've come up with." His previous geniality had vanished. He was now bent over the table with his hands folded together.

"I've a client to protect. Do you think I'd ever get any business if people thought I could be scared by any punk hood who comes along with a gun and some muscle?" Ellen was still silent with the two gunmen at the bar. None of her fright had subsided; her face was pure fear.

Damma gestured at Cass with his head. Cass moved away from the bar in my direction. He stopped and took my gun from his pocket, and then stepped in front of me, raising his hand with the gun in it to bring the barrel down across my face.

It was a momentary opening, and I had to take it. I brought my knee up hard into his crotch and stood up. He grunted and started to double up, and I brought my foot down hard on his. Then, as he yelled an oath, I grabbed his gun hand with my left and twisted his arm behind him while taking the gun with my right hand. Morton's gun was half out of the shoulder holster when I snapped off one shot, which took him in the shoulder and drove him back against the bar. His automatic thudded on the floor.

I pushed Cass onto the floor in front of Damma. Ellen's mouth was open as if to scream, but she stopped when I gestured to her to pick up Morton's gun. She did so while Morton muttered his first and only words of the evening, a stream of obscenities. Cass was doubled on the floor, moaning.

Through all of this Damma had remained seated with his hands folded in front of him. He got up and kicked Cass in the face once with full force. Cass's head snapped back and he groaned.

"That's enough, Damma," I yelled. "Get back and sit down."

He did as I said and folded his hands in front of him again. I stepped over Cass and stood behind Damma while I felt his sides. As I thought, he was unarmed. Ellen had moved away from and in front of Morton, who was propped against the bar holding his shoulder. To my surprise, Ellen was pointing his gun at him.

"A very impressive performance, Mr. Foley," Damma said. "These buffoons whom I pay well are obviously no match for you. Would you consider taking a job with me?"

I laughed. "I wouldn't like the working conditions. Now let's get this straight. My business and my client's is none of yours. From now on keep your God-damned thugs to home."

He smiled tolerantly. "Mr. Foley, we both want to know the same thing: what happened to the McReedy girl and why?" He paused for a moment and rubbed his hands together. "I should like to know, frankly, because if it is at all scandalous my associates can use the information. I'm inclined to believe that you know little more than I at the present. But why can't you have two clients, me and McReedy?"

"Forget about the ethics, Damma, and let's just say I don't like you and I won't work for you."

He shrugged. "Well, if you change your mind let me know.

Also, pardon my threats. They were designed to check on your protests of not knowing."

I moved to Ellen's side and took her by the arm. I put my gun back in its holster. As we went to the door she gave me the automatic. I removed the clip and dropped it in my pocket. When we got to the foyer, I threw the empty gun back into the bar. I heard the crash of glasses when we went out.

8

◌ THE SPRING chill of the evening air felt good when we hit the sidewalk. Ellen's heavy breathing was interspersed with sobs; she held my hand tightly in hers as we walked. I hailed a passing cab and gave the driver Ellen's address.

I put my arm around her trembling shoulders as we rode. After a few moments she lifted her head from my shoulder and took a handkerchief from her bag. She wiped her eyes and blew her nose, then sat back and turned her face toward mine.

"My God!" she said. "I've never been so terrified in my life!"

"You weren't the only one," I said.

"Are we in any danger now?" she asked. She was gradually becoming calmer and reasserting control over herself.

"I doubt it," I said. "He was trying to panic me into doing a job for him. But he and his friends don't really want any more trouble now."

She rested her head on my shoulder for the rest of the trip, and I held her against me to quiet the remainder of her hysteria. When we got to her address, I paid the driver and joined her at the door.

She turned to me then. "I thought for a while I'd never see this place again. Anyway, if you haven't eaten, come on up and I'll fix something. After a good stiff drink, of course!" she said with a laugh.

I smiled back at her and followed her inside and into the elevator.

"I really couldn't help it, you know," she said after the car had started on its way up. "I forgot to put the chain on the door—not that it would have helped much. They just crashed in with those guns."

"Don't worry about it," I said. "There wasn't a damned thing you could have done. Remember, we got out of it all right."

"Why do people like that want to know about Virginia?" she asked after we were inside and she was fixing martinis for us both.

I explained some of McReedy's union problems and how certain people would be able to use any items of scandal they might be able to unearth about him.

"How did they find out you were looking for her? Lord, it's not public knowledge."

"Damma has several good contacts within the police department itself. Particularly in the narcotics sections. My guess is he heard about us when the report of the Howards' party got to them."

"Why would they want to know about the party?" she questioned.

I detailed the use of informers and the role Randall was playing. For her edification I also discoursed on the need Damma had for police informers to protect his own important heroin operations.

"Randall? You must be joking!" she said when I had finished.

I shook my head. "No, what's to be surprised about? The poor guy was in a spot and they put the pressure on. There wasn't much else he could do."

She started to laugh. "You know, the Howards think he's great. He's straight down the line on all the things they accept: the war, drugs and all that. If they only knew!"

I emphasized again that no one was to know what I had told her. She assured me it would be kept strictly to herself.

She made us another pair of martinis and left me to enjoy mine in solitude while she went to the kitchen to put a dinner together. I glanced through a few pages of Howard's manuscript on her typing table. It was pretty much like the other things of his I had already seen. On the whole I was glad I didn't have to read the new one.

Ellen set a small dinette table on the kitchen side of the apartment and we went through ham and eggs and coffee.

"I plan to do some experimenting with recipes before summer school starts," she said. "Maybe you can try some more of my cooking."

She explained she would be teaching some freshman courses in a six-week summer session to help out with expenses while she worked on her Master's paper.

"I have a favor to ask you," I said.

"Fire away, sir," she replied. "I'm at your service."

"How can I get a look at Mrs. Howard's case file on Virginia?" I asked.

"Have you tried asking her?"

I related my afternoon discussion with her. "She acted as though I was trying to steal family treasure," I concluded.

"Not family. Hers. She really is a bitch, as I told you. Bright. Much brighter than her husband, by the way. But she's incredibly vain."

"What's this project of hers like?"

She related the nature of Sibyl Howard's work. She would take a subject who agreed to an intensive examination of his or her reaction to some shock. For over a period of a month or so she would have the person fill out a series of "in depth" questionnaires that were designed to measure changes in attitudes and behavior since the traumatic event.

"Does it work?" I asked.

"I don't know," she replied. "You'll have to read her book. Oh, there's a segment of it due to appear in the next issue of the *Journal of Critical Sociology*. It'll be out next month."

"I can wait," I said. "But how about Virginia's study? Do you know anything about it?"

"I know she did one last fall, but I've never read it." She paused and considered for a few minutes. "Here's what I'll do," she went on. "I'll have to leave some graded term papers in her office tomorrow. She won't be in all day, or so she told me."

"Don't take any chances and get yourself in trouble. You're not a full-fledged detective, you know. Is there any chance that she'll miss the file?"

"Oh, I won't bring you the original file. There's a Xerox in the library. It'll cost about a dollar and you can pay me from the petty cash."

"OK, but be careful," I said. "What time will you have it for me?"

"How about you meeting me here for cocktails tomorrow, and then you can take me to dinner in payment."

I agreed and stood up to go. "Look," I said, "don't worry about Damma now, and try to relax and forget the whole thing."

"I could do that better if you'd stick around. Like maybe for the night," she said and smiled.

"The idea's appealing," I said. "But I have some more work to do."

"Can I ask what kind of work?" she rejoined with a smile I could only call coy.

I related Irma McReedy's visit to me, and added that I thought it a good idea to inform her of Damma's interest in her daughter. There was always the possibility that she too might be bothered in some way.

"I met her last year," Ellen replied. "She seemed like a very nice person."

I thought for a minute. "You may be able to help after all. Suppose I take you to the hotel to stay with her. That way you can watch over each other on the odd chance something may happen."

"All right," she said. "If you won't stay with me, let's go. Just wait while I get a coat."

"Why don't you try your charms on some nice grad student your own age," I said while she went into the hall for her coat.

When she came back she was frowning. "Enough's enough. Let's drop it. OK?"

She was silent all the way to the car, and she remained so through the drive to the hotel. I circled the building a couple of times but couldn't locate anyone staked out there or following us. On our way through the lobby I continued to check; there were only the standard evening loungers occupying the couches and chairs.

I got Irma McReedy on the house phone and she asked us to come right up. She opened the door at my first knock. She was wearing a long wool robe. "Excuse my appearance," she said, "but I was just getting ready for bed."

We expressed our indifference to her dress, and she greeted Ellen with reserved pleasure. After Ellen and I were seated on the studio couch, I related our interview with Damma.

She had remained standing, but then she sat on the edge of the open, made-up bed. "Is there any chance, do you think, that they could be holding Virginia?"

"I doubt it," I said. "In the first place, it wouldn't make much sense for them to try to muscle me, if that's the case. But even saying that's a red herring, that isn't their style of operation. If it got out, it would fix the election for good as far as they're concerned and maybe do more than that."

"I'll call my husband tonight," she said. "You know, when I left him I pooh-poohed his asking me to keep things secret. I said he was acting like a child with all of his worry about people following us and all that. I guess I owe him an apology."

"I guess you do," I said.

"Do you really think we're in any danger now from Damma and those men?" she asked.

"As I told Mrs. Harris, I doubt it," I replied. "But it's hard to be certain. What I'd like to do is leave Mrs. Harris here with you just in case. She can get what she needs from the drugstore downstairs. I'll pick her up in the morning."

"Certainly," Irma McReedy said. "I'll be glad for some companionship and there's another bed here." She gestured at the couch on which we were seated.

"Good," I said. Ellen made a face with a downturned mouth when Irma moved away to the closet to hang up her coat.

I took the revolver from my shoulder holster and handed it butt first to Irma when she came back. "What's this for?"

"Just to have here. I hope as a conversation piece only. Have you ever used one?"

"Not on anyone. Years ago, when the Scheller strike was getting nasty, we kept one in the house and I learned how to fire it, if that's what you mean."

I nodded and she placed the gun in the drawer of her bedside table. Ellen followed me to the door, and as I went out her lips silently formed the word "Coward."

I checked the lobby again on my way out, but it was clear of any danger as far as I could see. Nor did the streets outside display any menace other than their usual quota, for that time of the evening, of decrepit alcoholics and occasional bands of roaming Negro youths. The center of the city at night was now their natural habitat. A few miles away, the daytime owners were shopping and entertaining in their suburban milieu.

Once in the car, I unclipped the revolver from under the dash and put it in the empty shoulder holster. It didn't seem a good idea to be unarmed for long. I drove at a leisurely rate to my apartment and made sure again that I was without a tail. For a while I thought of Ellen again and her offer, but the faceless image of a screaming college boy kept intruding.

Everything was quiet when I reached my apartment, and I was looking forward to a peaceful night of rest. I turned on the lights and tossed my jacket onto the sofa. A nightcap seemed like a good idea and I was on my way to the kitchen for the bourbon when my bedroom door opened and a man stepped out.

He was tall and lean with close-cropped brown hair tinged with gray. I was reaching for my gun when he said, "Wait a minute," and handed me another of the card cases. This one was identified as Jeffrey Corey.

"Christ!" I said as I handed it back to him. "Can't you people ever bother to knock?"

"Not if we can help it," he said with a fatuous smile.

"OK," I retorted, "as long as you're here, sit down and tell me what you're looking for. I don't feel like cleaning up again." I decided to let my drink wait and not waste good liquor on him.

We took seats, he in the easy chair and I on the sofa. "I hear you broke up some of Damma's boys tonight," he said.

"Your informers are good. I'll say that for you," I replied. "But what's it to you?"

"Not much. We're just trying to check on the McReedy girl and the union matters that seem to tie in with the syndicate." His voice was soft and rather oily.

"The last time it was CeeJay Jones you wanted to know about," I said sarcastically.

"You've sort of brought two lines of investigation into one," he countered.

"Do you think Jones is rigging union elections now?" I asked.

"Let's cut the humor," he answered with a frown. "Have you anything on the girl's disappearance?"

"For the second time tonight," I said, "no."

"Well, at least I'm not asking you the same way Damma did. By the way, I guess he's convinced you haven't got much information, but he's sure as hell mad at those thugs of his!" He laughed harshly.

"Good!" I said.

"He really wanted to scare the hell out of you, so you'd give him any dope you came up with."

I shrugged. "I can't say he didn't scare me," I answered.

"In case you're interested and can bury your prejudices for a minute, we haven't turned up anything either."

"That's too bad," I said. "As a taxpayer, I wish you could do something to make my work easier. But she seems to have done a good job of vanishing. Maybe she left town. I don't know." I kept Irma McReedy's information about the phone call to myself.

"We've run checks on the airports and the standard things, but nothing's turned up," he said.

"McReedy had some of his people do that too," I interjected, "and the trail, if there was any, was fresher then."

He stretched his long legs out in front of him and studied his well-polished black loafers. "Speaking of disappearances, our friend CeeJay will be pulling one in the next few days. I thought you might be interested."

I tried to show neither great interest nor surprise. "Since you know about it, I suppose you also know where he's going to vanish to," I countered.

He smiled knowingly and nodded his head. "We can guess his final stop, but he'll be going first to Texas and then across the border to Mexico."

"And then?" I asked.

"A plane trip across the Caribbean to Cuba, from there probably to the East." He sat back with a smug look on his face and crossed his legs.

"Where in the East?" I questioned.

"We haven't found that out yet," he answered. "Once he leaves this country, though, it's officially out of our jurisdiction. Then it's somebody else's baby." He looked as though this aspect pleased him.

"I have no reason to think he knows anything about the

girl," I said. I didn't know whether he knew about the marriage or not, but he wouldn't learn it from me. "His politics don't interest me."

He scowled and leaned forward in the chair. "Look, cities all over the country are going to blow to hell because of guys like that. Maybe you don't care, but we have to."

"Don't be so God-damned pompous," I retorted. "CeeJay Jones didn't make the circumstances that are causing the trouble. You've always got to look for communists under the bed."

His face became red and he snorted at me in disgust. "You liberal sons of bitches make me sick!" he said loudly. "Over forty years of commie subversion in this country and you God-damned bleeding hearts keep yelling civil liberties. No wonder the country's in trouble!"

There wasn't anything for me to say. I could tell by his grimace that any further discussion would be pointless. I got up and motioned him to the door.

"Now listen to me and listen good," I said. "I'm damned tired of you and your boys coming and going through my home and office any time you please. One more incident and, by Jesus, there'll be real trouble. Now get out of here!"

He said nothing more but only glared at me with a look full of contempt. I tried to appear equally disdainful, but I don't think I could have. Certainly I couldn't match his ideological fervor and self-righteousness. It took three drinks for me to stop being angry.

When I went to bed CeeJay Jones was on my mind, and when I woke up he was still there. After an early breakfast with four cups of coffee, I called Irma McReedy, who assured me that the night had gone fine without contact from anyone. She said Ellen would be ready when I came by for her, and I told her I might be an hour or so late but to have her wait for me.

I went down to the car and drove to CeeJay's storefront office. The street was quiet because of the light rain and wind that had sprung up during my drive. Here and there in the doorways of restaurants and pool halls a few men stood alone or in desultory companionship.

However, the door of the store was padlocked, and a crudely printed sign hung from the knob: SOUL BROTHERS—COOLING IT AWHILE. I rattled the knob a couple of times but this brought me no response. Back in the car, I sat a few minutes, considering Jones and his situation.

Finally I started the car and drove to a small tacky drugstore I had noticed while driving down. I pushed my way, through rows of shelves packed with merchandise, to the telephone booth. Here I phoned Ellen in Irma McReedy's room. She gave me the address of CeeJay's mother, and I told her to hang on, as I would pick her up before noon. Just to check, I phoned my answering service as well. The operator informed me that a Miss Violet Finch had phoned and left her number for me to call at my convenience.

I put my last dime in the slot, and her soft voice came through the receiver. "Why, Mr. Foley, I do appreciate your calling so promptly," she said.

"What can I do for you, Miss Finch?"

"Do you think you could spare me some time this afternoon? It's on a matter that's important to me and I would so appreciate your help."

I told her I would be at the campus later in the morning and could see her there. But she said she wouldn't be, and we set an appointment for two o'clock in my office.

I returned to the car and drove through the maze of twisted

ghetto streets to find CeeJay's house. It was on a narrow tree-lined street of old but sturdy shingled houses. Each house had a thin patch of lawn and a narrow driveway not designed for a modern car. Some of the houses were in good repair, with fresh coats of paint. Others were bedraggled gaunt structures with faded colors.

CeeJay and his mother lived in one of the freshly painted buildings. The house had a wide front porch furnished with a glider and a rocking chair. I rang the front bell and the door was opened by a tall heavy woman in her late forties. She was dressed in a simple faded house dress and bedroom slippers; her skin was light brown. She was holding a broom in her hand.

When I asked for CeeJay, she glared at me for a moment and then said, "He has the side entrance." Then she shut the door and retreated into the house.

I stepped back into the misty rain and took the concrete path at the side of the house. The side entrance door stood open and from within I could hear the sound of a tenor saxophone torturing a short melodic phrase. When pressing the buzzer got no response, I stepped inside and climbed a short flight of stairs to a closed door on which was tacked a large poster of Malcolm X making a speech.

I knocked on the door and CeeJay answered it. He was in his bare feet and had on gray slacks and a T-shirt. He didn't look surprised to see me.

"Hi, baby," he said. "Glad to see you. Come on in."

When I was inside, he shut off the small portable record player, and the room seemed unnaturally quiet with the saxophone silent. I saw the LP jacket of a John Coltrane record with the title *A Love Supreme*.

"You know, I was going to look you up today, honkie," he

said with a laugh. He threw himself down on an unmade cot in the corner. The room was sparsely furnished with an old kitchen table and some wooden chairs. There were two rooms beyond, but the doors were closed.

"What about?" I asked. I took one of the chairs and turned it around so that the back faced me and I could rest my arms on the top.

He turned and sat up, his bare feet on the floor. "I wanted to hear if you got onto anything about my wife," he said. "Man, ain't nothin' else I'd want to see you for. Sheet, no!" he sneered.

"I haven't found anything," I said. "Of course, maybe she'll just turn up one of these days, or she may never be found."

"Man, she had her chance with me. But now I'm going to be cutting out, baby. So you might say she blew it." He was frowning and he moved his feet back and forth and clasped and unclasped his hands on the edge of the cot.

"She's your wife," I said. I tried to show no curiosity over his announced departure. "But I presume it doesn't matter anymore as far as you're concerned."

"I guess I was wrong, that's all. She's just another of those mothering white chicks. Me, I got important business on now." He leaned his head to the side for a moment and then went on. "I'm going to make the international scene, dig?"

"Not exactly," I replied.

"Honkie, we're important now. Why should I waste my time worrying about someone who thinks I'm just some black stud?"

"Is that what she thought in Mississippi?" I questioned.

"Civil rights again. That's old shit, baby. Now we know where we are. White colonialism is through. I'm going to be with people now who're stopping it." His voice had an icy edge of hardness.

"She's still your wife," I countered.

"Individuals," he snorted. "They don't cut nothing now." He stood and paced back and forth on the bare floor and continued talking.

"Look, in two years we'll have every city in flames. Cats'll be blasting you mothers out of windows and behind trees. Nothing's going to be left: no cities, no suburbs. Nothing. You dig now, baby?" He stood close in front of me and raised his forefinger to simulate a gun and said, "Bang, you're dead!"

"In the meantime I'd still like to find your wife," I persisted.

"My wife. Sheeet!" he howled.

Then he went to the battered kitchen table and hoisted himself into a sitting position on its edge.

"I don't give a damn now, you hear? By tonight my black ass'll be out of here and away." His elation was apparent in the tense set of his figure as he sat with his feet swinging again and his arms folded across his chest.

"Do you want a divorce?" I asked.

"Makes no difference at all. That's what I was going to look you up to tell you before I went. You find the chick, you tell her I'm long gone. She can do whatever she wants. You hear me talking now." He threw his head back gleefully and clapped his hands one against the other in front of him.

"Divorce!" he yelled. "Oh, you bourgeois shits. All neat and proper in your suburban traps. Oh, you kill me!"

I could see that his exaltation was virtually limitless. He jumped down to the floor with a thud as his feet hit the boards. Then he resumed his prowling pacing about the room.

"Oh, man, respectability and hypocrisy. That's all you whites are made of. Murdering mothers!"

Then he turned and stood in front of me with his legs apart and fists on his hips. "What are you going to tell Virginia about me when you find her?"

"Not a damned thing," I replied. "It's none of my business. I'm paid to locate her, not to provide her with marriage counseling. You tell her whatever you want to."

"I may not even be alive long after I get back here," he said.

"When are you coming back?"

"What are you—a God-damned fink? Want to find out my plans and yell fuzz?"

"The way you blast your mouth off," I said, "you couldn't keep anything secret."

"The important things are secret, baby. But read the newspapers in the next couple of weeks." He paused. "And next year, duck when you hear something crack because it'll be me or someone like me trying to blast your mothering head off."

I didn't see any point in listening to any more. He was obviously keyed to the highest pitch.

When I turned to go he grabbed me by the arm and said, "You tell her for me, baby, she was right. Yes indeed, she was so, so right."

"I'm not your messenger boy," I said as I pulled my arm loose from his grasp.

As I walked away from the house, the sound of Coltrane's saxophone came dimly after me.

It was a little after eleven when I got to the hotel to pick up Ellen. When I knocked on the door, Irma McReedy opened it and asked me inside. She was dressed now in a bright flowered street dress. Her face appeared strained, and I doubted that she had slept well. Ellen was seated on the couch, and her appearance was also wan.

Irma McReedy asked me to take a seat for a moment, and I sat next to Ellen. "I talked to my husband last night," Irma said, "and he's going to fly in tomorrow morning."

"I'm not sure there's much he can do right now," I said.

"Maybe not, but the Damma matter upset him. He wants to do some more checking with his people here."

"OK," I said. "I'll get back to you here by tomorrow morning at the latest."

As we were going out to the elevator, Ellen said, "I'd just about given up hope of your ever getting here. By the way, here's your gun. I guess I won't need it." She took the weapon out of her purse and handed it to me. I dropped it in my coat pocket before the elevator doors opened.

On the way to the car I told her about my talk with Jones, again leaving out the marriage details. She didn't appear surprised at this, but she did when I told her about Violet Finch's request.

"I wonder why," she said.

"Well, I'll find out in a couple of hours," I replied. "Then I'll let you know."

"I have nothing concrete against the woman," she said. "I just don't like her."

"Your feminine intuition?" I asked.

She smiled but without conviction.

Ellen asked me to stop by her apartment first so that she could change her clothes and pick up the papers that she had to take to the campus. While she was changing I glanced at a copy of the student paper, *The Watchman,* which contained a piece on Violet Finch.

The article cited the good fortune of the school at being able to obtain the services of "the first lady of avant-garde theater in the United States." It chronicled her early career in the thirties as actress and director in the Theater of the Masses and her subsequent persecution and blacklisting at the hands of a reactionary Congress. She was still able, however, to maintain herself as a force in theater, even if on a clandestine basis.

I learned of her championing of Happenings and improvisational theater in the past few years. At the school she was expected to work further in the medium and thus get to the "nitty-gritty" of things and "expose the hypocrisy of the Establishment."

"A real ball of fire," I said as Ellen came back into the room. She had changed into slacks and a sweater and was wearing a raincoat. The misty rain outside seemed set for the day.

Ellen smiled and shrugged. "She's got a reputation anyway," she said. "Myself, I think she's a bore and a phony, but don't let me influence you."

"I never question a woman's judgment of another woman," I replied.

By the time we got to the campus the rain had begun to fall harder and the light wind had turned into gusts, which shook the tree branches with their delicate new leaves. I dropped Ellen at the Student Union and agreed to meet her at her apartment about six.

I was early for my appointment, so I picked up a cheese sandwich and some milk at the cigar counter and took them up to my office. As I was swallowing the last of the sandwich and sweeping the crumbs from my desktop to the wastebasket, my outer office door opened and Violet Finch stepped in.

She was dressed in a yellow slicker and was carrying a matching yellow umbrella. For a moment she stood at the entrance to the inner office with a quizzical look. I greeted her and gestured to the coat rack in the corner. When she took off the slicker, I was dazzled by a purple-and-green op art dress that seemed designed to give anyone who looked at it instant vertigo.

She sat in the client's chair and looked at me like a magpie sizing up the quality of a worm. On the whole, she seemed to find me wanting.

"What can I do for you, Miss Finch?" I asked.

"First, would it be presumptuous of me to ask if you have found any trace yet of that poor girl?" Her voice was soft and her enunciation precise and cold.

"Do you know her, Miss Finch?" I asked.

"No, no." She placed the negative with neat precision. "I've only been here three weeks and I've never had a chance to meet her. Paul and Sibyl have spoken of her a lot, and they are quite concerned."

"So am I, and her parents as well," I replied. "But to answer your question, no, I haven't found a thing that helps in tracing her."

"I'm so sorry," she said, and her words were tinged with pity.

"But if you don't want to see me about Virginia McReedy, what can I do for you?" I asked.

"Well, Mr. Foley," she said, "I suppose it's awfully nervy of me to try to take advantage of you. But when I heard from the Howards that you were a detective, it occurred to me that you might be able to help me."

"Do you want someone or something investigated?" I questioned.

She giggled for a minute and displayed an indecisiveness that didn't go well with her image of worldly femininity. "Oh, no, nothing like that, Mr. Foley," she said finally. "Actually I would just like some technical advice."

"I don't understand," I said.

"You see, I'm going to do a little didactic improvisation to open the summer school theater season on campus. I'm planning a piece on police brutality."

"Why ask me about it?" I said. "I'm not a cop."

She smiled hesitantly and then looked down at her neatly manicured hands, which were clenched tightly on the top of a small handbag with the same pattern as her dress.

"Oh, I realize that. But I did think you might have had some experience, that's all." The smile returned with more poise as she lifted her eyes and looked at me.

"I used to be a police officer, if that's what you mean," I replied.

"Yes," she said, taking me up at once.

"What kind of brutality are you talking about?" I asked.

"You know, the way you treat people in the ghetto and the way you beat confessions out of people."

"I don't," I said, "and I didn't when I was a cop."

"Oh, I don't mean you yourself, Mr. Foley. But what is it the police do?"

I laughed and pushed my desk chair back so I could cross my legs. "Miss Finch, for God's sake! What you're talking about is very complex. First, for Negroes the police are rough and everyone knows that."

Her eyes sparkled and she nodded her head in unison with my words. "Yes, but what do they do?"

"Nothing systematic, if that's what you mean," I answered. "It's more like sporadic low-keyed violence. Someone gets shoved or smacked up against the wall. Or a dice game is raided and the officer takes part of the pot and lets the game go on."

"I see," she said.

"But you've also got to see that these neighborhoods are left open to exploitation by the very nature of the city," I went on.

"Now you've lost me," she said with another smile.

"Well, it's like this: the respectable citizens need a source to get cheap labor from—housemaids, dishwashers, people like that. They get these people from the ghetto and let the police keep the natives in line."

I paused and studied her. She appeared self-assured as she drew herself back in the chair.

"Then," I went on, "the respectable liberals who need housemaids call the cops brutal fascists for doing their job for them."

"Liberals, that's right," she said and spat out the words.

"I was including people like yourself in that, Miss Finch. I don't see that you're much different."

She stood up and hit me flat across the face with her bag. Then she strode across the room, her shoulders stiff and straight, to get her rainwear. The door banged at her exit.

I sat quietly for a moment or so until the sting from the blow had subsided. Then I went to the medicine chest in my side room and looked at my wound in the mirror. The metal clip of her purse had taken a small piece of my cheek and left a trickle of blood. An application of iodine and a Band-Aid remedied it, and I took two aspirins to counter the headache.

I stood for a while at the window and watched the wind and the rain pummel the few pedestrians who were hardy enough to take them on. My thoughts ran to the missing girl, and the vileness of the weather made me conjure up all sorts of sentimental visions of someone lost and wandering in the rain with no place to go.

Finally I shrugged them off and got my raincoat out of the closet. By keeping close to the shelter of the buildings, I got to my car without any great damage. Once inside, I replaced the gun in the dashboard clip and made a mental note to clean the one Ellen had returned.

9

~ WHEN I got to my apartment, I poured some bourbon over ice and took the gun apart on the dinette table. It took about twenty minutes to complete the cleaning. I finished the bourbon and made myself another drink.

I felt restless and constrained, but I couldn't think of any place to break out to. My idea of Virginia McReedy was fairly clear; yet this clarity included no lead as to her possible behavior in the past two weeks.

I considered again resigning from the job and letting McReedy get someone else to find her. On the other hand, the case interested me because everyone involved seemed concerned about the girl. But this concern was coupled with no insight into her possible actions. Also, if she was in trouble, why didn't she get in touch with someone?

Finally I downed two more bourbons and took a two-hour nap. After this I had a shower and a change of clothes. My body felt better, but not my mind.

When I left to go to Ellen's, the gale was still sweeping its way through the city. The rain swept over the windshield and the wipers maintained a constant battle. The car radio announced that the entire lake front was being swept by heavy waves.

Ellen greeted me at the door with a martini in her hand. She was dressed in a black cocktail dress with a moderately plunging neckline that had its own attractions. Once inside, she placed me on the sofa, produced a footstool for my feet and a martini for my right hand.

"All the comforts of home from your assistant in crime detection," she said. Her mood seemed to be one of elation.

"I guess you got the report then?"

"Right you are and here it is," she said. She handed me a large manila envelope with my name written across the front.

Sitting down next to me, she placed her drink on the coffee table in front of the sofa, then turned to the side so that she was half facing me. I put the envelope on the table next to her drink.

"Thanks," I said. "Did you have any trouble?"

She shook her head. "No, but I had a close call."

"What happened?" I asked.

"Well, Sibyl's office was all clear, and I took the file and had it Xeroxed and replaced. No trouble."

"Seems clean enough," I replied.

"It was. But then I went to Paul's office to leave some pages for him. She'd just left on the way to her own office. We missed meeting by a bare five minutes."

"I'm sorry," I said. "It was a lot for me to ask." I meant it.

"No problem," she said. "A miss is as good as a mile. But what was interesting was Howard himself." She paused and took a large sip of her drink.

"What about him?" I questioned.

"He was crying," she said. "When I came in he was standing

by the window wiping his eyes. Then he said I'd just missed Sibyl."

I waited for a minute and then said, "Maybe he had a cold and his eyes were watering."

"That wasn't what he said when he grabbed me and tried to kiss me," she replied.

"He wanted sympathy?" I asked.

"He certainly did. The story was the standard one. His wife is a bitch and doesn't understand his side of things." She was smiling but there was a troubled look in her eyes.

"What did you do?"

"I gave him his papers and left," she said with an air of finality.

She looked at my face and asked, "What happened to you, by the way? Did you try to make out with Miss Finch?"

I described our interview and its violent conclusion. She laughed and said, "That will really fix you with the Howards."

"Why?" I asked.

"They're very close. As a matter of fact, it was Sibyl Howard who pulled the strings to get Violet Finch hired here." She paused for several seconds and went on. "The administration wasn't too keen on her, but Sibyl got together with some of the drama people and here she is."

"So I see," I replied, touching my cheek with my fingers.

We had another drink and then fought our way through the gale to a nearby French restaurant, which contained only a handful of diners. After a rather silent meal in which we concentrated mainly on the food, I took Ellen home and again declined an invitation on the excuse that I wanted to go over the Howard notes. It was true enough as far as it went.

The gale was going full force as I drove back, and I narrowly missed a large tree branch blowing across the road. With some feeling of relief then, I made myself some coffee as soon as I got in and settled down with Sibyl Howard's notes.

They were neatly typed in double space without other notations or corrections. The heading read:

ABSTRACT OF NOTES TAKEN ON V.M.

V.M.—21 years old

White

Female

Girl's father is a prominent trade union official. His income places the family in the upper middle class. However, as in many cases of this type, there are ambivalent status feelings (see below).

Father was educated in a free New York City college in the late thirties. He was an early foe of the American Communist Party. (N.B. He adopted social democratic ideas—espoused betterment of working class while not changing social structure to any extent.)

He worked as a laborer and moved up into trade union circles. During bitter disputes with the communists after World War II, he succeeded in brutally purging them from all positions of influence. He helped lay the groundwork for reformism in American life and, while fighting him ostensibly, helped the efforts of Senator McCarthy.

His vindictive attacks on the Soviet Union aided the neofascists in waging the Cold War against the socialist bloc.

He has followed a consistent pattern throughout his career. That is: he simulates identification with the underclasses, but his real class aim is to make them subservient to the interests of neoimperialism. At no time has he ever held out anything other than betrayal to the real interests of the oppressed in the West and the emerging forces of the Third World. He is anti-Castro and anti-Mao.

While he does not support the present Administration in its imperialistic attack on true democracy in Vietnam, he has, nevertheless, worked against the true forces for peace. He has boycotted marches and some of the teach-ins with red-baiting tactics.

In the same way, he campaigns for social reform on the race issue. He has criticized the advocates of the necessary violence. By the same token, he will not accept that a guerrilla war waged in the cities is the only cure for the American sickness.

For reasons given below, V.M. has been unable to emancipate herself from his influence.

Her natural mother deserted the father when she was a year old. No one knows the whereabouts of the mother. Evidently the mother was more truly radical, although this is uncertain.

The father obtained a divorce for desertion, and married his present wife. She was his former secretary.

His second wife, while only the graduate of a secretarial school, seems to have taken great care in raising the girl. V.M. feels toward her as to a proper middle-class mother. The stepmother seems to have shown no jealousy or antagonism when the daughter went through the classsic Oedipal phase. Indeed she appears to have encouraged V.M. in her attachment to the father image. As a result V.M. has adopted many of her father's social democratic values.

At an early age V.M. was told about her true mother's desertion of the father. However, so great was her attachment to her present parents that she has evidently never had any curiosity to pursue the matter further.

Certainly V.M., before her college years, had an unusually optimistic view of American society and what can be accomplished under its structural configurations.

As the subject was brought up in the classic liberal mode, she accepted her earliest sex experience while in high school without trauma. She lost her virginity while a senior, but the affair was short-lived.

During the early years of the civil rights movement she was, typically, active on the fringes in fund-raising, etc. The summer before last, she went to Mississippi as part of the summer project.

129

At first, she claims, she was shocked and horrified by the general atmosphere. The vicious violence of the whites did not frighten her as much as sicken her. She claims to have felt pity for the degraded circumstances of the whites themselves and their brutalization as human beings.

She argues that their violence cannot be changed without a change in their entire social system. With industrialization and unionization, she thinks things could, indeed would, improve in this area.

On the other side, she was genuinely upset by the behavior of many of her fellow workers. She contends that a sizable portion had come South merely as a gesture of defiance and to act out their own failures at adjustment. Also, she questions the security of their values since so many seemed more concerned with flaunting the mores of their parents.

In this connection, she was upset by the sexual exploitation that took place between the races. She feels that many of the Negro males deliberately set out to conquer as many of the white girls as possible.

However, on their own side, the white girls were, she claims, equally acquisitive in a sexual sense albeit not as perverse. They set out to take black lovers to atone for their sins of exploiting Negroes and to attain greater status in the movement itself.

She did not arrive at these conclusions immediately, she says, but as the result of some thought about her own experiences and feelings, as well as those of others.

Her first summer in Mississippi was spent in a voter registration drive. The unit with which she worked had targeted one county for development. They experienced considerable violence. V.M. herself was shot at several times and a homemade bomb destroyed one of their automobiles and its driver.

However, her most traumatic experience came when she was jailed as the result of picketing the county courthouse. Over half of her group was jailed at the time and several of them were badly beaten. Afterward there were two nervous breakdowns (both male) who had to be returned to their homes.

V.M. herself was hurt while in jail but only superficially, in a physical sense. The humiliation of the experience, however, tended to drive her even more into herself, and thus she came more and more to depend on her inner resources.

Undoubtedly, her interpersonal relationships would have suffered even more had she not met C.J.J. at that time.

C.J.J. is now a prominent black power activist and a student at this school. At that time he still accepted the cant of nonviolence. He too was beaten by the police and once, on the street, by Klansmen.

He and V.M. early entered into a relationship. Subject is reticent on the precise nature of their interpersonal encounter. But it was undoubtedly structured as a love affair.

The voter registration project was partially successful despite the fierce antagonism which they encountered. Several of the opportunist bourgeois Negro groups now control the black population there. Thus the good work led to reaction.

The following summer only a much smaller number of students went to Mississippi. V.M. and C.J.J., whose relationship had deepened, went together. They joined a group which was funded with Washington money, and was thus beholden to the neo-fascists.

Their object was to attempt to develop a cooperative workshop and school in their area and foster political activity. They entered the project with considerable enthusiasm. However, the imperialist reactionaries also came into the organization with the backing of their middle-class nationalistic parents.

As was to be expected, these fascist influences carried the day in Washington. C.J.J.'s faction was thrown out for improper use of funds and faulty bookkeeping. Thus, the retrograde forces were able to establish themselves firmly.

It was at this time that C.J.J. became a black power advocate. However, V.M.'s reaction was unstable. She evidently broke her relationship with C.J.J. and left him to carry on the fight alone. Bourgeois opportunism was triumphant over the emotional needs which C.J.J. had previously satisfied. V.M. does not discuss this at any length.

V.M.'s campus career has been equally ambiguous. Before she went South, she did take part in picketing the local Fox Motors plant. She felt this was a necessary task to achieve some measure of Negro fair employment in the area.

However, she withdrew from the picketing group when they scattered garbage over the steps of City Hall. Also, she refused to accept the lie-in, during which pickets placed their bodies across the road at quitting time. A heavy traffic jam occurred and twenty students were jailed. The lower-middle-class police, of course, behaved with classic fascist brutality.

At the same time, she would not go along with our petition to remove A.S. from the faculty. This reactionary professor of political science has maintained pro-Administration stands on the war. It is disgraceful that this man should be allowed to mouth a counter-revolutionary view under the pseudo-democratic slogans of free speech.

Similarly, V.M. has been opposed to the war in Vietnam on the grounds that it is futile. Nevertheless, she insists that the government of North Vietnam is equally unrepresentative and undemocratic. She criticizes the progressive forces among the students and faculty for supporting the true democracy of North Vietnam.

In recent months she has spoken out, in a letter to the student newspaper, against the booing of Secretary Gaither when he spoke here last fall. She considers this a failing of the progressive people to obscure elementary civil liberties. This girl still accepts the out-moded middle-class notions of John Stuart Mill.

Again, she does not believe that students should have the right to dismiss teachers. She does not see that the needs of the progressive students and professors cannot, in the name of history, be compromised by the antiquated ideologies of a dying social order.

As a student, V.M. has an excellent record. Her course work has ranged from political science and sociology to philosophy. Here again she has tended to favor the social democratic thinkers in all of these areas. She has been particularly scornful of such thinkers as Sartre, Marcuse and C. Wright Mills.

Incredibly, she still thinks in terms of a value-free social science in which the truth of progressivism is shackled by the false consciousness of the neo-imperialists.

She has recently tried her hand at writing of her experiences in the South. An article of hers in the pseudo-radical quarterly *Action* has been widely praised. Indeed, the article is not without merit but it is tarnished by its appearance in this organ of superannuated trade unionists and CIA supporters. She may, she says, continue this sort of writing.

She has taken some course work in philosophy with the husband of the writer. He has always been very impressed with the girl's ability.

However, in his classes this year, he has noticed an increasing degree of cynicism in her work. As would be expected, she has taken a line consistent with passé and vicious classical liberalism. She has, furthermore, begun to consider seriously the theories of elitism of such overrated men as Michels and Pareto.

The writer's husband tends to be more tolerant of these ideological faults. He stresses again and again the true abilities which the girl does have.

Nevertheless, in her other course work she has consistently chosen the courses given by the antiprogressive members of the faculty. Too, she has dropped all activity of an honest political nature. The truth about her is obvious.

While the writer has, together with her husband, extended hospitality to her on many occasions, this now must stop. P.H. is much too soft and relenting about this matter. All contact with her must stop.

It is obvious that in this case the girl's reactionary childhood and family have reasserted control as a result of the undoubtedly harrowing shocks which she sustained in the South from the whites. But these mitigating circumstances should not be given too much weight when we consider the very real danger which such people are to progressivism.

N.B. When the section dealing with this case is written, great care must be taken to see that the writer's personal feelings do not appear between the lines. For all of his pusillanimity and softness, P.H. may be able to check any lapses in this direction. He should be consulted.

It was ten o'clock when I finished reading the Howard notes. The wind was still engaged in its howling revolution outside, and the rain was pelting against the windows. While Sibyl Howard's animus was certainly confirmed by the notes, they didn't seem to advance my search very much.

I was considering whether or not to have a nightcap and turn in when my door buzzer rang. When I answered, I heard McReedy's voice asking to come up. A few minutes after I pressed the buzzer, he was seated on my sofa. He appeared haggard, as though he had had little sleep since I had last seen him. His eyes were desperate.

"I didn't think you were coming in until tomorrow," I said.

"I managed to get a plane late this afternoon," he replied. He paused and looked at me uncomfortably. "Look," he said, "I'm sorry about the danger I got you into with Damma."

I shrugged. "That's one of the risks of the job. You can't tell at the start what you're going to be involved with."

He studied me carefully before going on. "Anyway," he said, "I'd like you to take this as a bonus or whatever you'd like to call it for the risks you're taking."

He stepped over and handed me a check, then returned to his seat. I glanced at the amount, which was five hundred dollars.

"It's not necessary," I said.

He shook his head emphatically. "No, no, I want you to have it."

I put the check in my pocket and returned my attention to him. "The syndicate boys seem quite interested in your life," I said.

"That's why I've got to carry this election," he replied. "That scum is just waiting to be able to move in and I think you know what it would mean."

I nodded.

"Dummy locals," he went on, "yellow contracts, the works. Christ, I've got to stop it!"

"How do things look now?" I asked.

"Fifty-fifty," he said. "We may be able to swing it. But it's going to be close."

"Shouldn't you be working on that end, then," I suggested, "and leave this part of things to me?"

"This Damma business scared me," he said with what was supposed to be a smile.

"Well, I wouldn't worry about it too much," I replied. "You knew anyway that the syndicate is interested in the election."

"I didn't think they would be throwing their muscle around yet!"

I laughed. "They're always ready to do that if it's necessary. What happened was they thought they could frighten me into working for them and you at the same time."

"For what?"

"Anything I found out about Virginia—and they hoped I'd find something discreditable, you can be sure of that—I'd pass on to them as well as to you."

"The bastards!" he said.

"They're businessmen of a sort," I went on, "but the thing is I got out from under before anything happened. Now everybody knows what they tried, and I'm pretty much useless to them."

"If you say so," he replied.

"The only legitimate gripe I have against you," I said, "is your not telling me about the phone call from Virginia."

His face flushed and he averted his gaze from mine for a moment. Finally he looked up and asked, "Could I have a cup of coffee, please?"

We remained silent, he in his seat, I in the kitchen preparing the coffee, until I brought the cups in from the kitchen and sat down again.

"You're right, of course," he said. "You should have been told."

"If you don't feel you can trust me, you should never have hired me," I said harshly.

"It wasn't you, you see," he went on. "My first marriage is something I've always been ashamed of."

"Why?" I asked. "She left you, as I understand it."

"True, but you always wonder," he said and then broke off.

I waited while he fidgeted for a moment and had some more coffee. Then I said, "The point is, it was important for me to know."

"I thought you might be able to work on the affair, turn up Virginia, and her mother's name wouldn't have to be raised again." His voice was pitched lower than was his custom.

"I don't understand," I said.

"I want her mother kept out of this. It's important. You've got to understand that."

"Why?"

"Because I've built my own name and reputation completely apart from my first wife. She can't be brought back now."

He frowned, then asked, "Have you found any trace of her mother in this?"

"No," I replied, "but from what your wife said, she seems involved."

"She can't be, that's what I'm trying to tell you. She's dead!" he blurted out.

"Are you sure? I thought you'd had no contact with her and didn't even know where she'd gone to."

His gaze was directed now entirely at the floor as he scrutinized it between his wide-spread knees.

"That's what everybody thinks, even Irma," he said finally. "I knew I'd have to tell you this. That's why I had her stay at the hotel when I came over here."

"Do you want to tell me now?" I asked.

He waited again and then said, "No, but I guess I don't have a choice, do I?"

"It's up to you," I said. "But sure as hell, I'm not going to get anywhere on this job unless I know what it is I'm doing."

He sat back against the sofa cushions then and started to talk. Rita McReedy had been devoted to him at first. She was intelligent and poised, but most of his union work at that time had kept her in the background. McReedy himself was aware that she wanted to take more of a part in things. But the day-by-day pressures of organizing and faction fights left little place for her talents. So she became increasingly dissatisfied.

He hadn't lied when he'd said he had no idea where she went when she left him. At the time he hadn't. But ten years later, when he was already happily married, he had received a letter from San Francisco sent to him personally at union headquarters.

It was from Rita. The letter outlined her reasons for leaving him and how she'd later realized that these were inadequate. She wasn't asking to return to him or anything like that. Basically all she wanted him to know was that she regretted it all. She had read about him and his new wife and hoped they would always enjoy happiness. As to Virginia, she would always feel guilty about her.

After she left him, she'd assumed a new name informally. San Francisco had been her initial destination and she had remained there through the years. She and Morris had parted company after a year.

She returned to school and took a degree as a librarian. This had provided her with a steady job at one of the local colleges. Even though she had left McReedy because of her isolation, she led a very withdrawn life in California.

However, this had changed when she fell in love with a student there who worked on a part-time basis in the library. Evidently it had been a one-sided affair because he broke it off after the first two months.

This had hurt her, she said, but she was able to adjust to it. But the shock of finding herself pregnant had not been taken into account in her resolutions.

She told the student nothing about this development. Rather, she made contact with an abortionist on her own. The operation had been successful, but she had developed peritonitis.

When she wrote McReedy, she was dying in the hospital and had wanted him to know. She asked for nothing and did not intend to disclose her identity as she knew a scandal would hurt him as a public figure.

McReedy had gone to San Francisco on the pretext of union business so that Irma need not know. However, Rita had already died and been buried.

"So you see," he concluded, "Virginia has no natural mother to get in touch with her."

"I'm sorry," I said, "but you see, I had to know."

He nodded. "I'd rather no one else did and not just for my public image either. Although I can't deny that that's important."

I assured him of my discretion.

"But how about it, Foley. Are we getting anywhere?" he went on.

"I'll be honest with you," I said. "I haven't come up with a damned thing that points to anything concrete. I've checked everything here among her friends, but I haven't found a single thing that's any good."

"What's next?" he asked.

"I don't know," I replied. "I'll keep digging for a couple more days among these people, but after that I'll just have to give up."

"That doesn't help me," he said.

"No," I continued, "but it doesn't help to take your money without any results either."

"Stay on it for at least another week, Foley. Please." His voice was almost a direct cry for help.

"I'll think about it," I said. "At least I'll try to work up some new track anyway."

He stood up to go. I offered to drive him back to his hotel or call a cab for him, but he had come in a rented car. When we parted I agreed to join him and Irma for dinner at their hotel the next evening so that we could talk out some new approaches.

As I got ready for bed, I had to admit to myself that there didn't seem to be anything new to be done.

10

MY ALARM went off at eight and when I got up, bright sunlight was drifting through the window and reflecting back at me from the dressing table mirror. I glanced out the window and saw that the only remains of the storm were a few slowly drying puddles and scattered branches torn from the trees by the wind.

I went to the kitchen and put the coffee on while I did the usual things with the frying pan, the bacon and the eggs. The silence was a little oppressive and did not go well together with my own state of depression about the McReedy case. So I turned on the radio and after several bars of Sinatra and some early-morning disc-jockey talk, I heard it.

It was the morning news on the half hour, and the nasal announcer related the discovery of a young girl's body swept up on the lake shore in Clancy Township. The body had been discovered by a boy walking his dog on the beach. Nothing more was said and the voice went on to a Far East crisis.

I decided to let a cup of coffee substitute for breakfast. When I got Ellen on the phone her voice was hazy and thick with sleep.

"Can you come out to the lake around Clancy this morning?" I asked.

"Is this a fast proposition or what? My God, if it is, you pick the worst hours!" she said and laughed.

"I can't join in the humor now," I said and felt rather pompous. "It's business and it may be a little grisly. Are you game?"

"I'll be ready in half an hour," she said and hung up without further comment.

I had a fast shave and a shower, which took up about twenty minutes. When I got to Ellen's she was waiting for me on the sidewalk, dressed in a sweater, slacks and loafers.

"You're late, chief," she said.

I frowned and started up as soon as she was inside.

"You really are in a hurry, aren't you!" she exclaimed after a glance at the speedometer.

I told her about the radio broadcast I had heard.

"You think it may be Virginia?" she asked.

"I don't know," I replied, "but I've got to check it out. Also I want to get it done before the McReedys hear about it and get upset, perhaps over nothing."

"You're right," she said.

"By the way," I went on, "in any case the body won't be a pretty sight after being in the water for over two weeks. You're going to have to try and identify her if you can. Do you think you can take it?"

Her face paled for a moment and she turned away to look out the window. "I'll do my best," she said finally. "Now I am really scared!"

We drove in silence for a while and then she said, "Did you find out much from the notes?"

"Only that Sibyl Howard certainly hated Virginia," I replied. "I presume she kept that out of the finished study."

"She'd have to. But of course I haven't seen that part. The full manuscript's at the publisher's and she keeps the copies of that at home."

We were again silent until we neared Clancy Township. It's not really a town, although there is a one-story frame city hall, a few stores and a couple of churches. But basically it's simply the designation for an area of cottages, estates and beaches that dot the lake shore. In the winter, only the year-round residents with their homes far enough back from the water to avoid too much dampness are in evidence. However during the season the cottages and beaches are packed beyond capacity with summer residents and vacationers, hot dog stands and carnivals.

I took the expressway route for speed, which cut us off from any view of the lake until we swung into the lake highway, running parallel to the water. The sun was a bright yellow cloud in the sky and it cast a haze over the now calm water.

When we came to what there was of the town proper, I pulled into the suboffice of the county sheriff, which was housed next to the city hall. The deputy was on duty. Tom Moore and I had met several times previously. He informed me that the body was being held for identification and autopsy at the township hospital, five miles farther out; he said he would call ahead that we were coming.

The township hospital is a neat brick building four stories in height. It is surrounded by green well-kept grass and beds of tulips. On that day it was resplendent in the sunlight, and the flag lay limply on the staff for lack of a breeze. As we pulled into the parking lot at the side of the building, I noticed that Ellen's face had paled again and her hands were clenched into tight fists on her lap.

"Take it easy," I said. She turned to me with a wan half smile but said nothing.

We walked up the tulip-lined walk and into the administration anteroom. A prim middle-aged woman behind the information desk directed us back to the emergency intake area, where the town morgue was located.

When we got there, a gnarled white-coated attendant had to summon the doctor on duty before we could try to identify the body. The doctor bustled in, took our names and addresses and the reason for our request.

Finally we convinced everyone that we were legitimate. The attendant drew one of the drawers open from the cabinet on the far side of the room. Fluorescent lights then beat down more heavily, it seemed, on the battered body that was disclosed when the sheet was pulled back. Two weeks in the water had indeed taken their toll and the result was difficult to view.

Ellen gave a gasp and put her hands to her mouth. She nodded her head and turned to me with tears welling in her eyes. I took her by the shoulders and led her outside, where the doctor was waiting.

I told him to call the coroner's office and advise him of our identification. He didn't want us to leave, but I insisted I would have to go to bring the girl's parents. It was out of the question to leave Ellen, as she was close to hysterics. As I took her down the hall to the exit, her shoulders were shaking and she held a handkerchief tightly to her eyes.

She sat in the corner of the front seat in silence as I drove out of the parking lot. When I came to the main lake highway, she turned to me and asked, "Are you going to phone the McReedys?"

"No," I replied. "I'd better tell them about it in person. They're going to be hurt enough without getting the word over the phone."

She said nothing more. It was about a ten-mile drive to the expressway entrance. I was hitting around sixty and almost missed the turnoff. But I made it in time, and as I turned onto the entrance ramp I saw the legend on the signboard standing a short distance up the highway itself. It read: "STAY AT THE CLEARWATER MOTEL—5 MILES AHEAD—ROUTE 8."

I had no time to read any further for I was busy trying to follow twists and turns of the ramp. It seemed that the first real break had come too late to be really profitable.

However, there was no time to do any checking then. I wanted to get to the McReedys before they heard of the body's discovery from the papers or radio. It was a Saturday morning, so the expressway was relatively uncrowded and we were able to make good time.

As we moved into the city traffic, Ellen stirred and glanced at me. "My God, what could have happened to her?"

"Drowning probably," I answered. "Anyway, there'll be an autopsy and a coroner's inquest. It'll all come out then."

"Are you going to tell the McReedys?" she asked.

I nodded. "I'll have to see they get out there when the man from the coroner's office does," I went on. "I'd like you to go with them too."

"Do I have to?" she asked. I could see the tears beginning to form in her eyes again.

"No, but I'd appreciate it. I think her parents are going to be pretty broken up over this and I could use some help."

"OK, I'll do what I can," she said. She continued to sit far to the side in the car and returned to scrutinizing the traffic and pedestrians as we drove.

"Do you think it was murder?" she asked finally, turning to look at me again.

"I don't know. We can't tell anything at this point."

We reached the hotel, and I jammed the car into a narrow space in front of a no parking sign.

"Should I come up with you?" Ellen asked.

"Please," I replied.

Without further ado, she climbed out and waited for me to come around to the sidewalk. It was just a little before noon and the sun was heating the air. I could tell it was going to be a hot spring day, but it seemed cold as death, and I was sure the McReedys would feel that way too.

I took Ellen's arm and steered her into the hotel. She walked hesitantly, as if she were not certain to find support for her feet. The hotel lobby was barren of people, save for a few reading the early-afternoon papers in the main-floor seats. I glanced at the front page of the paper at the newsstand, but I could see no report of the body.

I didn't bother to use the house phones. We stepped into the first elevator and went immediately to the McReedy's suite. He had told me of their change when he arrived and had given me the new room number.

Frank McReedy opened at my first knock. He stood in the doorway, wearing shirt and trousers without a necktie. I could see his wife sitting at a room-service table on which the remains of a brunch stood. She too was dressed, but I could see her feet clad in bedroom slippers under the open table.

"Foley, come in. We didn't expect you until tonight." He stood back and motioned us into the room.

I introduced him to Ellen, who went over to an easy chair on the side of the room nearest to Irma McReedy. He sat down next to his wife while I remained standing in the center of the room. They all looked at me. I felt like hell.

"She's been found," I said. I thought desperately of some easy way of putting it, but there wasn't any.

"Where is she?" Irma asked before I could say anything more.

I looked at Ellen but she lowered her gaze to the floor. "Her body's at the coroner's office in Clancy Township," I said.

McReedy just sat staring straight at me, and Irma McReedy gave a gasp and knocked over a coffee cup, spilling brown liquid over her green dress.

"No, no," she mumbled.

Ellen stood up and placed her hands on Irma's shoulders from behind. Irma was seized with trembling and then Ellen led her to the sofa against the far wall. She held Irma McReedy in her arms as the sound of her sobs seemed to possess the room.

McReedy clenched his jaws and I could see his eyes become angry even as the tears formed. He pushed his chair back and went into the bathroom, from which I heard the sound of water running. Finally he came back and stood facing me.

"What happened?" he asked.

I related the radio broadcast and the trip Ellen and I had taken to Clancy.

He turned to Ellen. She was still holding Irma, whose sobs were now subsiding to low groans. "Are you sure?"

She nodded and continued to stroke Irma's shoulders. "Yes, I wish I thought there was any chance I was wrong, I swear to God I do, but I'm not." Her voice was barely above a whisper.

"Jesus, what happened?" he asked. Then he turned and glared at me, waiting for me to tell him how and why his daughter had died.

"I don't know yet," I replied. "But I've got an idea."

"Tell me your idea then. God damn it, man!"

"Not until I know what I'm talking about," I said. "I've got to check further; then you'll know."

"Listen, I'm paying you. What happened?" He was nearly screaming into my face now, and I thought he was going to hit me. I braced myself to catch a blow I wouldn't be able to return, but he turned and took his seat behind the brunch table.

"Be reasonable," I said. "She's evidently been dead for over two weeks. Probably shortly after you last heard from her. There wasn't much anyone could do. Not you, not me."

He shook his head pensively and stared at the dirty dishes. "I know, I know," he said. "I'm sorry, it's just the shock." Then he put his head in his hands to hide his crying. I felt like joining him.

Irma McReedy turned from Ellen's arms and amazingly enough smiled at me. "Please forgive us, Mr. Foley. It's just so terrible."

"I understand," I said. "This isn't particularly easy for anyone."

"What do we have to do?" she asked.

"First you'll have to go to Clancy and identify the body. There'll be a man from the coroner's office and he'll want you to sign some papers."

McReedy got up and went to the bedroom and Irma followed him. "Just a minute and we'll be ready," she said as she left.

Ellen looked at me and said, "This is terrible, terrible."

We said no more until the McReedys returned. Then I said,

"If you still have your rented car, I'd like Ellen to go with you. She can show you where to go."

"Where will you be?" McReedy asked.

"I've got to try and find CeeJay Jones," I replied.

"What's he got to do with this?" McReedy demanded.

"He's her husband," I said. "He has a right to know. I don't know if I'll be able to find him because he's leaving town shortly. But I've got to try."

McReedy and Irma looked at each other and then back to me, their faces blankly interrogating me. "When?" she asked.

I explained the marriage as well as I could and my reasons for remaining silent about it.

"We had no idea," McReedy said. "Actually we've only met him twice, I think. Does he have anything to do with this?"

"Not as far as I can determine," I replied.

They agreed then to go with Ellen. I said I would bring CeeJay back with me if I could. However, in any case they would wait for me at the hospital.

"Please hurry," Irma said.

I said I would.

I drove rapidly through the now thickening Saturday shopping traffic. The ghetto area streets were now packed with throngs of shoppers and the inevitable male bystanders in their usual watching posts along the sidewalks. There was an air of sad festivity about the comings and goings of the pedestrians.

I pulled up in front of CeeJay's with no other witnesses than two small boys playing with a large toy engine on the walk two houses down. First I went to the side entrance, but the door was locked and my knock brought no response. After a few minutes I went to the front door and rang the bell.

The same woman came to the door and looked at me quizzically. She was dressed now in an old-fashioned housecoat which zipped up the front. It was a faded light blue and ragged at the sleeves and neck.

"CeeJay's not here," she said.

"Will he be back or has he left?" I asked.

She shook her head. "Not yet," she said. "If you want to come in to wait, it's OK. He should be back in a few minutes."

She stood aside in the doorway so that I could go in. I stepped into a dark foyer with a closed closet at the side behind the door. There was a short flight of three steps and I entered the parlor.

It was a large room with a smaller dining room opening off it. The furniture was old but sturdy and the chairs and sofa were covered with bright floral material. Light penetrated the room from the porch windows, and I could see motes of dust dancing in the sun's rays. Cotton curtains were hanging at the windows but were pulled aside to give the light entrance.

The dining room was lighted by two wide windows that looked out upon a narrow strip of backyard and the back of the house on the parallel street. A heavy oak table covered with a crocheted cloth stood in the center of the room. To the side was a sturdy buffet, on top of which stood two silver candlesticks.

There were several pictures on the living room walls: one of a small boy in short trousers standing in front of the house, a faded portrait of Marcus Garvey and a splendid candid shot of Mahalia Jackson, arms spread akimbo and an ecstatic look on her face bent back in exalted song.

"Take a seat, please," she said in a voice neither friendly nor hostile, but neutral in its distrust.

"I'm sorry to disturb you," I said. "It is important though." I took a seat in a large upholstered rocking chair.

She took a seat in an overstuffed chair opposite me and next to a portable TV. Then I noticed two battered leather suitcases with straps fastened around them, which stood in the far corner by the dining room.

"CeeJay said you could be trusted," she said. "Is there some trouble?"

It wasn't my place to tell her about her son's personal life, and I had no way of knowing how much she knew about him and Virginia. "A friend of his has had an accident," I said.

"You mean Virginia?" she questioned.

I nodded.

"What happened?" she asked.

I told her, still leaving out any reference to her being CeeJay's wife.

Her face drew up and her eyes darkened. "You know, she was my daughter-in-law."

"Yes," I said.

"You may not believe this, but it's going to hurt my son so much."

I remained silent, and after a moment she went on. "I didn't approve, not at all. Then the way she abandoned CeeJay and all. But she was a nice girl, and I'm sorry. I just hope my boy won't mourn too much and hurt himself. He loved her, you know."

Before I could reply, I heard the sound of steps on the front porch. A minute later CeeJay stepped into the parlor. He was dressed in a neat blue suit and he seemed to be in a hurry, from the pace of his walk.

He stopped at the side of the room next to his mother's chair and looked at me questioningly.

"Man here has something to tell you, son," she said. "I'll be in the kitchen if you need me." She stood up and walked through the room to a swinging door at the end of a short hall by the side stairs.

After she had left, CeeJay glared at me and sat down. "What the hell do you want now?" he asked.

"I've got bad news, CeeJay."

"Well, lay it on me, man. Bad news is something we've been used to for a long time now." He leaned forward in the chair with his hands placed tightly on each knee. His face was impassive.

"Virginia's dead," I said harshly. His face twisted in a contortion of rage and grief. He stood up and turned his back to me.

Finally he turned and looked directly at me; his impassivity had been restored. "How?"

I related the details again. Each time I told the story it became more and more oppressive and senseless. "Also, I've told the McReedys about you and Virginia."

"That was none of your business." His tone was agitated.

"They have a right to know now," I replied.

"You're right," he said with a sigh. Then he sat down again and studied the ends of his shoes. "Was it suicide?"

"I don't know yet," I answered. "I still have some work to do, but I should know by tomorrow."

"Tomorrow! By then I'm supposed to be in Mexico," he said and raised his head to confront me directly.

"That's up to you," I said. "I thought you should know. What you do now is your business, none of mine."

"What do you think I should do, man?"

I laughed. "Don't ask me. You're a big boy and she was your wife. How can I tell you what to do or how to feel?"

"I really don't understand. It wasn't because of us. I know that," he said.

I was glad that the situation seemed to have stopped him from using his black power jargon. It was the only thing there was to be glad about.

"I can't say yet," I said.

"I can. When we stopped seeing each other she wasn't glad about it, that much I know. But she was a hell of a long way from wanting to kill herself. Believe me or not."

"I do," I said. "As far as I can tell, you had nothing directly to do with it."

"Nothing. Direct or indirect, and that's the God's truth. Maybe I didn't always act like it, but I loved her."

"I believe you," I said. "She probably felt the same way, if I understand her at all."

"You never knew her."

I nodded in agreement. But the past few days had brought me, in an indirect way, close to the girl. I thought I had a good idea of the way she thought and felt. Certainly as much as anyone else I'd met recently.

"True," I replied, "but there are other ways of knowing someone."

He was quiet for a moment. Then he said, "OK, what do we do now?"

I said that I was going back to Clancy to meet the McReedys. If he wanted to go with me, he was welcome.

"I'll come," he said. "Just let me see my mother for a minute and we'll be set."

"I'll wait," I said.

He went out through the door into the kitchen, and I could hear the sounds of a whispered conversation. I was unable to make out anything that was said. I didn't try.

On the way out he talked quite a bit. For the most part, he simply reminisced about his wife: her courage, skill and wit.

It was the first time I was completely convinced of the strong feeling they must have had for each other.

"How will this affect your trip?" I asked him.

"Well, man, I guess it can just wait for a few more days until we get this straightened out. Don't you think?"

It wasn't really a question, but I nodded anyway.

"Yeah, some cat's been in Mexico a week now and a couple of days extra won't hurt at all."

"By the way, do you think anyone could have hated Virginia?" I questioned.

"Hated? Hell no, she was a quiet girl and didn't mess with anybody if they didn't mess with her first." He turned and smiled at me to emphasize the point.

"That's how you feel, but how about the other people who knew her?"

"Are you suggesting that someone killed her?" he asked in a tone of astonishment.

"I'm not suggesting anything, only asking, that's all."

"Well, of course, I can't say too much about her ofay friends. A lot of them call themselves radicals, but underneath they're the same old white liberals like they always have been. You dig?" The question was without hostility.

"Anyway," he went on, "I didn't see much of those people. Especially in the last two semesters. But I don't know of any reason they should have anything against her. Why, she was their friend after all."

I didn't pursue the matter any further because we were in sight of the hospital. There were fewer open spaces now in the parking area, but I managed to locate one close to the door to the emergency area.

We went inside and when we got to the morgue section, we found Ellen and the McReedys seated on a long oak bench

11

⌒ I HEADED the car out to the lake highway. There were large and small motels scattered along the route. Since many of the travelers preferred to stay on the outskirts of the city, motels had sprung up in an almost geometrical progression in recent years. Their clientele tended to be vacationers coming to or passing through the city and salesmen and other business types who wanted a pleasant room with modern conveniences without the frustrations of city hotels.

I soon spotted the sign for the Clearwater Motel, which advertised a Paul Pine lodging recommendation, a bar, a restaurant with gourmet cuisine and a swimming pool. While the gourmet cuisine was obviously a palpable lie, this would not matter to the typical guest and he would probably get a good bed and his money's worth.

Five miles farther down the road I saw the motel itself. The center area was a three-story structure with an office, a bar on the second floor and a restaurant on the third. From this two wings radiated, each with about twenty-five doors and carports. In front of the building was a large swimming pool surrounded by a punctiliously kept lawn. At the side of each wing a walk led back to the beach, and there was a long jetty that extended some fifteen or twenty feet into the lake.

At that time of year the swimming pool was not yet in use. But it must have presented a gleaming vision of affluence in the summer nights with lights directed on it from above and the tourists frolicking in carefree luxury. The hippies would have called it a symbol of depersonalization; I called it simply tasteless and useless. But then there was the lake pollution.

There were few cars in the lot, and I had noticed that most of the carports in front were empty. The place had an eerie feel of ultramodern desolation.

I parked the car and walked to the edge of the parking area. A flight of five steps went down to a walk that led to the jetty. It was bordered by a grassy lot with maple trees and shrubbery that partially obscured the view of the lake.

I strolled along the walk to the other end, where another flight of stairs led to the beach. As I walked along I could feel the sand seeping into my shoes. I reached the jetty and walked out to the end. It was about twenty feet long and protruded out over water that was lapping gently at the pilings.

I stood for a while gazing at the water. I had the place entirely to myself. The heat was strong now and the sharp sunlight ricocheted off the water and dazzled the eyes. I thought about how it must have felt to Virginia to sink into that water.

After ten minutes or so I retraced my steps to the parking lot and went around to the office. I walked into a plush modernistic lobby with fixtures vaguely reminiscent of bad Leger and Bauhaus.

I took an elevator to the second floor where there was a large room with tables, a bandstand and a large circular bar. The room was surrounded with glass on all sides, which provided a view over the lake and the highway.

The place was sparsely populated, with a couple of middle-aged business types in conversation at one of the tables, and two women engaged in postluncheon intoxication at the bar. I sat down on one of the bar stools and waited for the bartender.

When he saw me, he came over with speed; I could imagine his tip quota was sagging. He was a short pudgy man with thick fingers and a knowing look on his face. I ordered a bourbon on the rocks.

He brought it back to me and I handed him a dollar bill. As he turned to go to the register I said, "Wait a minute."

He turned back and asked, "What can I do for you, pal?"

I held up a ten-dollar bill and the snapshot of Virginia McReedy. "It's yours," I said, "if you can tell me anything about this girl."

His eyes glinted greedily and he took the photo from my hand. I held on to the ten.

He studied the snap for a couple of minutes and then nodded his head slowly. "Yeah, yeah," he exclaimed forcefully. "I remember her."

"What about her?" I asked.

"I don't know much. Couple of weeks ago, on a night with about as many customers as we got now. Anyways, she came in about nine or so and she just sat here for about three hours drinking Scotch." He stopped and looked at the ten like a hungry wolf.

"And?" I asked.

"That's all. I only noticed her because it was a slow night, and she didn't look like the type to work at drinking like that."

"Did she say anything?"

He pursed his lips and shook his head emphatically. "Not a thing. Just kept ordering drinks. Didn't bother anyone."

"Was she a guest, do you know?"

"I couldn't tell you, pal. You can ask downstairs."

I handed him the ten and he pocketed it and moved toward the women drinkers and their thirst.

I finished my bourbon and headed back to the elevator. When I got down, I went over to the registration desk. A neat fussy-looking young man attired in a faultlessly pressed blue suit and a russet shirt looked up at me.

"Can I help you, sir?" he asked.

I said I'd like to see the manager and when a questioning look appeared on his face, I flashed my identification. Without saying anything more, he turned and went through a thick plain door in the back.

When he returned he was accompanied by a heavy-set balding man in his late forties.

"Will you come with me?" the manager asked cordially.

I followed him into a neat office with a large window that gave a fine view over the lake. He sat down behind a flimsy-looking modern desk and looked across at me as I sat down in an eggshell-shaped chair.

"What do you want? Don't try to make any trouble." The cordiality was gone from his voice.

"I'm not here to make any," I countered. "I'm on a missing person job; I don't do divorce work."

"Sorry to sound nasty," he said. "But in this business, scandal can do a lot of damage."

I took the photo of Virginia from my pocket and handed it across the desk to him. He took it and studied it for a minute or two. Then he got up and went out the door.

I studied the lake again until he came back with the desk clerk.

"I recognize her," he said. "She came in on May second with another woman, who had registered earlier in the day. They had the room for one night. On the morning of the third, the girl came in and said she'd take the room for another night."

"Did she pay in advance?" I asked.

"Well, that's the thing," he continued. "The older woman paid for the first day in advance. Next morning the girl came by and said they'd take the room for an extra night. So I just stuck it on a bill, figuring they'd pay up next morning."

The manager cast him a look that could safely be called baleful.

"Then what?" I questioned.

He looked apologetically at his boss. "Next morning they were gone. Just the girl's bag left in the room."

"What name were they registered under?"

"Mrs. Rita McReedy and daughter," he answered.

"What did the older woman look like?" I asked.

He described her as in her late forties, small and wiry, with bluish-white hair.

"Do you recall what kind of car she drove?"

"A Volkswagen, I think," he replied.

"One other question," I said. "Do you remember the home address they used?"

"Some place in New York City. I remember the bill, though, because I had to pay the last half of it." He glanced sideways at the manager, who lowered his eyes.

"Thanks a lot," I said, and at a nod from his boss he left the room.

"I'd like to get the bag," I said.

"That's a little irregular."

"I'll pay the balance of the bill, so the guy's loss will be made up," I countered.

He went out again and came back with a light leather overnight case with the initials "VM" stamped in gold on the top surface. We shook hands, and I parted with twelve dollars.

On the way out I stopped at the registration desk and told the clerk his boss had some money for him. He thanked me and looked self-righteous.

I put the bag in the back seat of the car and headed out toward the city. As I drove, I turned on the car radio for the two-o'clock news. After word from the national service on the Far East crisis and a plane crash in Oklahoma, the local announcer took over and related the discovery of Virginia McReedy's body. The voice described her as a local student and the only child of the nationally prominent labor leader; it went on to note that the exact cause of death was as yet unknown.

I stopped at my apartment and took the overnight case upstairs with me. When I got inside, I tried the case but it was locked. It took only a few seconds with a convenient burglar's pick to open it.

Inside I found two light dresses neatly folded, underwear and cosmetics. There was a pair of high-heeled shoes wrapped in plastic in the bottom at one of the sides and a paperback copy of *Aspects of Revolt* by Max Nomad. Stuck in the middle was a letter in an ivory-white deckle envelope.

The envelope was postmarked April 21 from New York City. I extracted the letter inside and unfolded the sheets. It was written in a neat spidery hand without a date:

MY DEAR VIRGINIA,

I realize very well how surprising this letter is going to be to you. After all, you have had no knowledge of me in your life. Real knowledge, that is.

I debated with myself for a long time before writing you. I thought how upset you will be, if you decide to come to know me.

But there are deep sources of mother love which cannot be denied.

So, in a way, I must ask your pardon for thrusting myself into your life when so many years have passed already without my presence. However, even without me, I'm sure you have grown into a remarkable young woman. For only a person of sterling character could have been as brave and upright as I understand you have been.

Actually, I first learned of your courage and nobility when I read about you in the papers two years ago. Even then, I considered trying to get in touch with you. I went to the library and checked your number and address from your local telephone directory. Then I wrote you a long letter which detailed my life since I last saw you as an infant.

But when it came to mailing it to you, my courage failed me. I thought that you might reject me, and I couldn't stand to take that chance. The thought of encountering any further personal coldness from those I love and who should love me is too much for me to bear.

However, I have finally summoned up all the courage at my command to ask you to see me and get to know me. Please, my dear daughter, do not refuse me this solace. When you learn what has happened to me in this life, I am sure you will find it in your heart to forgive me.

As to myself, my dear, the years since I left you have been harsh to me. I say this because the fault is really not mine. It is difficult to attempt to apportion blame in human relations. They are, to some degree, beyond our control.

However, I must insist still that there are standards of human decency and care which we cannot relinquish without some blame attaching to those who do so. It is only because I feel so morally secure in my position that I have been able to retain my sanity throughout the years.

But you must also understand that fear is a terrible thing. Now that I have used the word, I must acknowledge the reality of the thing it stands for. Yes, it has been a very real basic fear that has deterred me for so long. I cannot lie to you again. My rights were once taken away, and even the thought of being in such straits again terrifies me.

I must be confusing you terribly, my dear. Nevertheless, there are things I still do not want to put into writing. In the first place, you might very well not be willing to credit the truth of my account were you to see it in bold form on paper. Secondly, the things which frighten and shame me would do so even more in such form.

Therefore, my daughter, I will be driving to your city in another week. It is vitally important that you allow me to see you. I can only plead and say please, please.

Also, do not, I beg of you, tell anyone about our plans. The reason for this will be apparent after you have heard my story. But do know and understand that I mean you no harm. What damage has been done to our natural relationship was not of my doing.

If you agree, please phone me collect at 212 MU1-9177. We won't be able to talk long, but we can make arrangements.

Your loving mother,
RITA

I folded the letter and put it back in the envelope. Another search of the overnight bag disclosed nothing else, and I closed it and placed it in a corner. The McReedys would want what was left of their daughter.

I dialed the long-distance number given in the letter. After talking to two operators, I learned that the number had been disconnected and that, no, there was no way of learning to whom the number had been assigned. However, they did inform me that there was no Rita McReedy listed in any of the directories for the New York boroughs. It didn't surprise me, but I wanted the confirmation.

It was then three o'clock. I phoned the Clancy sheriff's office, and Bill Haynes told me the autopsy results would be available in a couple of hours. We arranged to meet in his office at six. For the rest of the time, I could only wait.

I put in a call to the McReedys' suite. Ellen answered and I told her it would be later in the evening before I got back to them. Also, I asked them all to wait for me there, because I wanted to wrap everything up.

"You sound pretty calloused," she said in a low tone.

"I don't like anything about what I've got to do now," I replied. "But evidently someone has to do it."

"I'm sorry," she said. "Make it when you can. We'll wait for you."

I hung up and went to the kitchen to stir up something to eat. However, food had no attraction for me and I ended up by mixing myself another bourbon on the rocks.

Then I returned to the living room and put some Mozart on the turntable. The sounds filtered through the air gently, but they couldn't take away the dead girl's battered face in the eye of my mind.

Around five o'clock I roused myself and made coffee and a couple of ham sandwiches. They had no particular taste, but they served their purpose.

With Daylight Saving Time in effect, the twilight hour was still bright as I made the drive back to Clancy. The air was becoming clear and chilly, and the lake waters were tranquil. At that time of day traffic was light and I got to the sheriff's office shortly before six.

Bill Haynes was expecting me. His coat was off and a silver-handled .38 was prominent in his belt holster; he was standing by the back window with a coffee cup in his hand. When I came in, he turned and gestured with the cup toward the coffeepot on a rickety table at the far side of the room.

"No, thanks," I said.

He remained standing with his back to the window. "Some of the boys from the local press were out," he said.

I sat down by the table with the coffeepot. "That's their job," I replied.

"We didn't let on that the McReedys were in town," he went on. "But they'll find that out soon enough."

"That's OK," I said. "It can't be helped."

He moved over to a battered rolltop desk that was stacked with old posters and forms. After he sat down and turned his chair to face me, I asked, "What about the girl?"

"Full report's not in yet," he said with a grunt. "But from what they tell us, it's a simple drowning."

"No possibility of violence?"

"There's always the chance. You know that." He stopped and laughed at me. "However, there are no marks on the body that are out of order with being in the lake for a while. No wounds or unusual cuts."

"How about rape?" I asked.

"Nope," he said and wagged his head back and forth. "She wasn't attacked."

"Poison, anything like that?" I questioned.

"Not a trace, John. You can't make a murder out of it, if that's what you're getting at."

"It's not," I replied. "I want to make sure, though, that I know what I'm doing."

"You know as much as we do now. If you do come up with anything, we have to know." His tone was cold and firm.

"I wouldn't cross you," I said. "As far as I can see, what I'm after doesn't affect you. If it does, I'll yell."

I got up and walked toward the door. "By the way," he said, "some federal people were out asking questions about Jones. I shouldn't tell you, so you don't know where you got it from."

"I'm not surprised," I answered. "Thanks a lot, Bill."

"You can do me a favor sometime," he said as I closed the door on my way out.

12

⟋◦ I STARTED the car and headed out onto the lake highway; I decided to take the longer route back into the city and skip the expressway. The extra distance would give me some time for thought, and the work that remained to be done on the case didn't fill me with much enthusiasm.

I drove past the Clearwater Motel, which now was vibrant with colored neon lights and red arrows that pointed the way to turn in. A few cars were scattered around the premises, but on the whole the display seemed wasted.

When I got into the city I pulled up in front of the first drugstore I came to. The telephone directory provided me with the Howards' number. I swung into the booth and inserted the required dime.

Sibyl Howard's voice answered with a thin hello and I identified myself.

"Mr. Foley, we've only now heard the news. Paul and I are heartbroken," she said.

I assured her that they weren't alone in their feelings.

"Is there anything at all we can do?" she asked.

"If you can spare me a few minutes," I replied, "I'd like to stop by for a talk. There are a couple of things you may be able to help me with."

"Tonight?" she asked, and a hint of surprised disdain crept into her voice.

"If it's at all convenient," I said.

"We are planning to go out later this evening. But if you can come by now, we'll have some time."

I said I would be there in half an hour and hung up.

On my way to the suburbs I drove by the university. There were a few lights in the buildings, but the overall atmosphere was one of somnolence. A lighted bulletin board in front of the Administration Building announced the start of the summer session in three weeks.

It was just becoming dark when I parked in front of the Howards' house. A full moon was rising and beginning to cast a cold lacquered light over the well-trimmed lawns and shrubs of the area. The coach lamp in front of the house was lighted.

Shortly after I pressed the doorbell, Sibyl Howard opened the door. She was dressed to go out in a neat tailored suit with a skirt slightly longer than was fashionable.

I followed her into the living room, which was dimly lighted by one floor lamp. She perched herself on an ottoman in front of an overstuffed chair and motioned for me to sit where I liked. I chose a straight-backed chair directly across from her. There was no evidence of Paul Howard.

"My husband's upstairs dressing," she said. "He'll be down in a minute. Tell me, do her parents know yet?"

I explained that they were in the city.

"Please tell them, won't you, that we are very upset. We'll try to call them tomorrow. Whatever happened, do you think?" She was seated forward with her elbows on her knees and her chin propped in her knotted hands.

"I thought you could help me with that," I said.

"Me? But what would I, or my husband for that matter, know about it? I don't understand." She had wrinkled her brow and put a questioning look in her eyes.

"Tell me, why did you do it? I think I know, but I'd like to hear it from you."

"What are you talking about? Surely you're not implying that we hurt the girl or anything like that!" A tone of petulant exasperation was now obvious as she spoke.

"Oh, I know you did nothing to her physically," I said.

"I don't know what it is you're insinuating," she snapped, "but whatever it is I don't like it."

"Neither did Virginia McReedy," I said.

"If you're going on with this insane talk, I'm afraid I'll have to ask you to leave. You can be sure I'll inform Mr. McReedy about the way his employees act. There are libel laws." She stood up then and started to move toward the door.

I remained seated. "What I was going on to say was that Virginia surely didn't like being the victim of the hoax you perpetrated. Even though she wasn't aware of it."

She turned and sat down in the overstuffed chair and pushed the ottoman away with her feet. "Hoax? Are you insane! I've never had to put up with such nonsense in my life! Just for laughs, what hoax are you talking about?"

"The hoax I'm talking about, Mrs. Howard, was having Violet Finch masquerade as the girl's mother," I replied.

"You really are insane, Mr. Foley," she countered. "Really, you have a surplus of nerve!"

"I have a letter in Miss Finch's handwriting," I said. "If we have to, I'm sure a handwriting test will confirm it as being hers."

"Miss Finch. How am I responsible for what she might do?

That's not to say I credit your fantastic story for an instant."
Her intonation now was harsh and the words came out rapidly.

"Come on now," I said. "My guess is that when you did
a study of Virginia for your work on humans under stress, you
found out a lot about her."

"What if I did?" she asked. "It's a scientifically valid ap-
proach."

"Yes, but hear me out in my madness," I went on. "So you
had some idea of what her weaknesses might be. Then too,
Virginia appeared to be an ideological traitor from your point
of view."

"What!" she exclaimed.

"You though of her as representing reactionary tendencies.
So when you had set Miss Finch up to come here and join the
staff, you also asked her to help you in a little practical joke.
I'm presuming you didn't intend all of what happened."

"You can't prove a bit of this and you know it."

"I don't have to prove anything," I continued and I was
pleased to note her growing anger as evidenced by the grimace
she wore for a smile. "There hasn't actually been a crime. I'd
like to know what was the precise story Miss Finch told Virginia before she abandoned her there so she could get drunk
and fall or jump off the dock."

"My God, what gall!"

I continued. "So let's say, as a hunch, she told her something
to upset her, then she left the motel on some excuse, promising
to come back and get Virginia and they'd go away for a few days
together. But she didn't return, of course, and Virginia
cracked."

"Now really, Mr. Foley!" She went on and used a tone one
would use on a troublesome mental patient. "Virginia was our
friend. Why, we'd have been ashamed to meet her ever again

when a joke like the one you're describing was over. And Violet! She'd have been certain to meet her on the campus."

"But you didn't care what happened after it was done," I said. "You were going to break relations with her anyway. If she had said anything to you, you'd have only laughed at her for being so vulnerable and gullible."

She stood up and went to the bottom of the stairs; she looked up and called, "Paul, come here at once!"

She waited at the foot of the stairs with her back turned to me and one hand clenched tightly on the banister. I heard a series of rapid steps from above and then Paul Howard emerged, coming down the stairs.

"What, Sibyl?" he asked. Then he paused when he saw me. Finally they both came into the living room. She resumed the seat she had vacated, he stood by the side of her chair. He was dressed except for his tie and coat, and he exuded an odor of talcum and shaving lotion.

"What do you want now, Foley? We've tried to be decent with you all along, even while you've been snooping and spying. Now you're getting everyone upset again. What is it with you anyway?"

"Cut the tough talk, Howard. In my record, both of you rank pretty high as sons of bitches, so don't try the indignant put-upon act. You know why I'm here."

"Paul, he really thinks we planned some sort of bad practical joke on Virginia. He's accused us of getting Violet to masquerade as Virginia's mother and of driving her to suicide."

"You've got a hell of a lot of God-damned nerve," he said and stepped toward me.

"If you want to start rough stuff, Howard, I'd be glad to oblige," I said. I didn't get up. I only wanted to end the act.

He stopped and stood for a moment indecisively and then

said, "I've no intention of dirtying my hands with a cop. Get out of here."

I stood up to go and said, "OK, but it will all have to come out at the coroner's inquest, you know. McReedy'll see to it."

He really looked scared. His face went slack and he balled his hands into fists. I thought he might be going to cry.

"Paul," Sibyl said. It was just the name, but the meaning was clear.

He shifted his attention completely to his wife. "See what you've done," he said.

"Shut up, Paul!" she exclaimed.

"No. You've ruined everything now," he retorted. "My fellowship, career, the works, just for one of your bitchy ideas!"

She jumped up and slapped him across the side of his face. "Will you get control of yourself?"

"No!" he shouted. "I'm tired of doing what you want done, the way you want it done. You killed that girl as surely as if you had pushed her into the water yourself. It was your bright idea to say McReedy had put her mother in an asylum."

"Oh, my God! Now you've done it good!" She sighed with obvious disdain and exasperation. "Why not go and call the newspapers and give them a statement? Maybe you can do a TV interview while you're at it."

She remained standing, glaring at him with palpable hatred. He returned her look, but his arms were beginning to tremble. They had both forgotten my presence.

"Tell me you're not a malicious bitch!" he screamed.

"And tell me you're not a coed-chasing bastard! You were dying to get that little fink in the sack with you."

"That's a lie. And you never had any proof she was informing to the police."

"Proof! Jesus, that's good! The fuzz are busting kids all over the place and she's making noises like a manure-eating traitor. You want proof. Mr. Hot Pants, that's what you were!"

"So you had to kill her," he said.

"Stop that nonsense. I didn't touch her. It's not my fault she was such a weak little twit she couldn't even hold up her own ego. You make me sick, you half-assed philosopher!"

They stood in angry confrontation. He kept his arms at his sides, and she stood with her arms folded across her breast, looking up at him.

"Paul, I'm through," she said finally. "I've had all of your cowardice and skirt chasing that I can take!"

"And I've had all of the emasculation from you that I can take!" he snapped back.

"All right. All right, you crud. I want you out of this house and I want you out tonight." Her voice was firm and tightly controlled.

"I live here too," he spluttered.

"Oh, Christ, it wasn't me who took your balls. You never had any to begin with," she said; then she stepped around him quickly and went to the foot of the stairs.

As she started to mount them, she looked back at him and screamed, "You make me sick. You're disgusting!"

He stood and watched her ascend the stairs. When she had passed out of sight, he turned to me and gestured for me to sit down. I went to the chair again, and he took the seat his wife had vacated.

"What can I say?" he asked.

"There's not much," I replied. "All the harm's been done."

"I didn't intend it. From the beginning I was opposed to the whole idea." His hands were trembling and twitching as he held them on the arms of the chair.

"So why didn't you stop it while there was still time?" I asked.

He looked over his shoulder at the stairs. "I couldn't control her. She insisted Virginia deserved it. She claimed that Virginia was responsible for the police raids for pot. Then, too, she thought Virginia was a reactionary. And also I guess she was jealous of me."

I couldn't see why, but I asked, "Did she have grounds?"

He looked at me for a moment and ran his tongue furtively across his lips before answering. "Not actually. I was tremendously fond of Virginia."

"Yeah," I said, "everyone should have such friends."

"I suppose you're right," he went on, "but I didn't have anything to do with this myself."

I kept silent. Finally he asked hesitantly, "How much of all this will have to come out publicly?"

"I hope every God-damned bit of it," I replied. "You people played fast and loose with that girl. She's dead as a result. You really accomplished something. Yes, you did."

I got up and walked toward the outer door. He followed me and raised his hand to my shoulder as if to stop me. I pushed him aside and opened the door.

"Please tell her family I'm sorry," he said.

I slammed the door as I went out.

I sat in the car for a moment before starting it. The forthcoming meeting with the McReedys and CeeJay was one I would gladly have missed. But there was no way of avoiding it.

I drove through the suburban streets and back out to the main thoroughfare. The Saturday-evening traffic was becoming heavier as the cars crept along to the outlying restaurants and theaters. A few flocks of shaggy-haired teen-agers were walking through the gigantic shopping plaza that serviced the Howards' area. A Saturday night like any other, except for Virginia and those close to her.

When I got into the hotel I stopped in the bar and bought myself a drink. With the weekend, the well-heeled bar trade was doing its drinking in the suburbs. A funereal air clung to the few people in the hotel bar, and my bourbon tasted like long cold ashes.

McReedy opened the door himself when I rang. His face was haggard, and he said nothing when he saw me. He just held the door open for me to pass inside.

Ellen was seated in one of the easy chairs paging through a news magazine. On the sofa CeeJay was stretched out, his face an impassive mask. They stayed where they were, and McReedy followed me in and stood over me when I sat down.

"Irma's sleeping," he said and pointed to the closed bedroom door. "She was on the brink of collapsing, so I gave her one of my pills."

"Have the papers called here yet?" I asked.

He nodded as he took a chair just across from me. "I told them I'd meet with them in the morning when I had something to tell them. I was waiting for you."

Ellen was watching me closely, but she remained silent, with the magazine suspended in her hands. CeeJay had not moved since I came in; now he turned his head and looked at me sullenly.

"What can you tell me?" McReedy asked.

"Was your daughter a good swimmer?" I countered.

"Not very," he answered. "She could swim a little, but she never cared for it very much. Now, what happened?" His voice had an imperative ring.

"She had an accident. That's the best way to put it," I replied. "She was weak in certain places and some people played on those weak spots.

"Look," I went on, "there's a marginal area in some acts. On the one side is clearly honest behavior, on the other, criminal. What happened to Virginia is in the shady area that doesn't quite cross the criminal edge."

"OK, but what happened?" McReedy insisted.

I detailed my reconstruction of the circumstances that had led to her death, including the scene I had witnessed and participated in at the Howards'.

When I was through, McReedy sat back in his chair and lowered his gaze to the floor. "I see," he said. "The bastards!"

CeeJay got up from the couch and went to the door. At my questioning glance he only said, "See you, boy," and went out. I didn't try to stop him.

Ellen said, "I can hardly believe it. It seems so silly."

"I know," I replied, "but that's the way it happened. Whether Virginia was drunk enough to have fallen into the water accidentally or whether she was just tired of everything and jumped, we'll probably never find out. I don't even see that it makes much difference."

McReedy still said nothing for some moments. When he did, it was only to say that he would let Irma sleep and tell her the story in the morning. "What can she do now anyway?" he asked rhetorically.

"I know it's no comfort," I said, "but I'm sorry. She seems to have been a fine girl." The words sounded false and hollow in my own ears.

McReedy had relapsed into silence and continued to sit, looking blankly at the carpet. "Let's go," I said to Ellen.

He got up from the chair and followed us to the door.

"Thanks for all you've done," he said. "Please send the bill to me here."

I said it was all covered, and we went out.

As we came out of the elevator and into the lobby, Ellen took me by the arm and said, "I could certainly use a drink. How about you?"

I nodded assent and we went on into the darkened bar and took a small table in the back and at the side. We stayed in silence until the waiter had returned with our drinks.

"Was all of that the truth?" she asked finally.

"As far as I can find out, it is," I replied.

"But what on earth could they have said that could have upset her so much?"

"All I know is what Howard said about the insanity thing. My guess is they came up with some cock-and-bull yarn about McReedy blackmailing his wife for a divorce by having her shut up for a while."

"But that's silly!" she said.

"Not really," I went on. "People have had relatives locked up as insane because they didn't get along."

"But that's so vicious," she said. "Not only that. It's fantastic!"

"We know that, but consider the way it was done. Surprise was the main thing. Virginia was contacted and presented with a mother she'd never even seen and hadn't much thought about."

"They caught her off balance," she interjected.

"Sure. Remember, Sibyl Howard had dug pretty deep in her interview. She'd found out some of the girl's weak spots and she put the pressure on them."

"And the main weakness was her father," she added.

"Right. She managed to cast doubt on her father's integrity, and McReedy's supposed to be a very honest man indeed."

"Wouldn't Virginia have questioned it at all?" she asked.

"Yes, but Violet Finch is an experienced actress, a pro," I said.

"But why did she abandon Virginia there at the motel?"

"She had to break it off some way," I conjectured. "That was the way it would hurt the most. You see, the thing was designed to beat the girl up as much as possible. So after upsetting her with the story, Violet probably said she had to go out someplace and would be right back. Instead she just vanished again."

"That would be quite a shock, I guess," Ellen said.

"Evidently it was enough to send her out drinking and from there into the lake."

Ellen grimaced and gave a shudder with her entire body.

"It wasn't very pretty," I went on. "But it certainly was even more effective than they counted on."

"Oh, it seems so petty and so foolish!" she exclaimed.

"Also," I said, "you've got to realize that Sibyl had a good set of motives for doing what she did. First, she suspected Virginia of informing to police about drug use."

"Sibyl never said anything to me about it," she said.

"She wouldn't have," I answered. "Hell! She probably didn't trust *you* too much, for that matter, but at least you weren't muttering what she took to be reactionary ideas."

Ellen smiled rather palely and took a sip of her drink. "I see," she said.

"Then too," I continued, "there was Paul. From what she said tonight, I gather he had made some passes at Virignia, and Sibyl found out."

"You mean like he tried with me?" she asked.

"Sure," I replied. "I think he was scared out of his wits by his wife and he was looking for whatever feminine kindness he could find.

"And, too, don't forget that she was doing that research into human behavior under stress. So she could justify it to herself as scientific research in case she had any doubts about the ethics of it."

She sat in apparent thought for a few moments while I finished my drink. Then she asked, "But what about Violet Finch?"

"What about her? She was indebted to the Howards anyway for helping to get the job for her. In her case also there were additional reasons. Certainly, from what I understand of the sort of theater she goes in for, she'd be very interested in an improvisation like this."

She resumed her pensive study. "What happens now?"

"There'll be the inquest. I don't know how much of this will come out. But there's nothing to question about the death. It was definitely accidental. The body was probably tangled in the pier foundation until the storm tore it loose."

"I'm sorry for everyone," she said as we stood up to leave. "These poor people with their degrees and animosities."

"I suppose so," I said.

On the way to her apartment we both sat lost in our personal meditations on the death and the people whom it affected.

"What will happen to us all?" she said finally.

"We'll get on just like everybody else," I replied.

I took her upstairs in the elevator and left her at her apartment door. She didn't attempt any further humor or display any affection toward me. I was tired and so was she. When I turned to leave she asked me to call her, and I said I would be in touch. I liked her, but the job was over and I was too old and, in some ways, knew too much to make it likely we would see much of each other. Nevertheless, it was nice to have known her, even with the disadvantages.

As I drove home, my fatigue began to gain on me. I wanted nothing better than a shower and a good night's rest. Such were my intentions, at any rate, when I pulled into my parking area.

The evening air had become chilly and the moon bathed the walkway with its soft light. However, I neither heard nor saw anything until I felt the prod of something in my back.

"Let's go back to the car, baby!" The voice was CeeJay's.

"What the hell are you up to now?" I snarled.

His first reply was another jab with what I now took to be a gun. When I turned to face him, I saw it was a .32 revolver. Then he said, "You're going to help me get out of here, man!"

I looked at the gun and then at his face, which was worn and drawn as though he were recovering from the effects of some intense emotion. But the gun in his hand was held steady at my stomach. "OK," I said.

We walked to the car. He stayed behind me and stepped into the back seat, still keeping the gun pointed at me. I could have moved on him then, but I was too damned tired. So I climbed behind the wheel and turned to face him.

"Where to?" I asked.

He said nothing for a moment, and then he ignored my question to ask one of his own. "Baby, do you know what I just now did? Oh, man!" He chuckled with a nasty sort of glee.

"I'm not sure I care," I said. "But for the record, what?"

"I shot that Howard bitch, man. Yes indeedy, she ain't going to screw up any more blacks' wives!" His laugh was now a sneer of self-righteousness.

"When?" I queried.

"Oh, about an hour ago. Cab dropped me off. I rang the bell, and when she opened up, bang!"

He moved to the corner of the seat diagonally across from me and rested the gun in his lap.

"Did that help anybody?" I asked.

"Help? Who cares. Sheet, you honkie creeps walk around and take everything away from us, and we're supposed to be good fuzz-headed darkies and pardon you. That sort of crap is over, man, you hear?" He leaned forward and thumped the top of my seat with the barrel of the gun.

"Yeah," he went on as he sat back again, "as soon as I heard your story, I went out and got me a cab right over to the Howards and did what I had to do."

"What goes now with your trip? I presume you're not going to go to the station and hand in your gun." But I knew what he would do.

"Why, baby, I'm cutting out of here right now, but quick. You dig?"

"And how am I supposed to help you?" I asked.

"You can give me some bread and drive me out to the freight yards." His voice was soft and faintly mocking.

"Good enough," I answered. "But you know I'll have to call the police when you go. I'm still enough of a cop to have to do that."

"Sure. But one hour is all I need. How about it?" He was not cajoling or threatening now; he was asking.

"Why not?" I replied. "Still, everyone's going to be out after you. I don't think your chances are too good."

"And what would they be if I stayed?" he countered. "You know what the press and the commentators will make out of it. No, I'll make it to Mexico if I can." He sounded determined.

"You've got a point," I conceded. "I suppose you already know you won't only have the regular police to worry about. The federal guys will be out in force too."

He roared out a laugh that resounded through the enclosed space of the car. "Man, they're the worst. You think other fuzz are hypocrites—you should have seen those bastards in action! Christ, the crackers are honest anyway. But those guys with their hearts for the rednecks and their orders to help us!"

He was silent for a moment and then went on. "They can try for me any time, any place. Let's go, baby."

I started the car and pulled out into the city streets. The late-night traffic was sparse for a Saturday night, and I made good time. We went across the city and through the downtown area.

The main freight yard loomed up in my headlights after about fifteen minutes of driving in silence. I pulled into a dark side street by the yards. There were no street lamps but the moonlight disclosed clearly the general layout of the tracks and the staggered groups of boxcars.

"Here we are," I said.

He looked up at me as I turned in my seat to face him. "How about the bread?" he said.

I took my wallet from my hip pocket. He watched me closely as I did so. It contained fifty-some-odd dollars, which I handed to him.

"Thanks," he said and shoved it into his pants pocket. Then he moved out the door on the side away from me.

"For what it's worth, good luck," I said.

He laughed and said nothing. The last I saw of him, he was walking across the tangled sets of tracks, moving quickly and lithely. I started the car and headed back to my long-delayed sleep.

I didn't get my sleep right away, nor did I get to call the police about CeeJay. Shortly after I got home, I was visited by a homicide detail about the Howard killing. Not wanting to be an accessory and for other reasons, I kept my knowledge to myself and pretended surprise. My only contribution was to tell them about the McReedy case. They were already looking for CeeJay.

A few days later CeeJay was shot to death in the rail yards in a small Texas town. The police claimed he had pulled a gun on them when challenged. Later I heard from some of the homicide boys that his gun was in his belt unfired. But the newspapers never reported it that way, although they were sensational enough.

The McReedy inquest finally declared the death accidental, but not before all the facts came out. Howard resigned from the faculty, semi-involuntarily. At last word, I understand he is working in one of the California think tanks for democratic inquiry or something like that.

I saw Ellen only once afterward. That was to take her to the airport to fly out for a visit to her parents. She never came back, and the last I heard from her she was arranging a divorce and planning to marry an attorney in San Francisco. She had gone to work in his office as a stenographer and was now going to join the firm permanently.

McReedy won his election, just barely, but a win anyway. He sent me another five-hundred-dollar check as a bonus. I didn't argue; I deposited it.

At the end of the summer Violet Finch telephoned and

castigated me royally because her contract had been canceled for reason, she claimed, of the publicity. Anyway, she blamed me for killing Sibyl and sticking my nose in where it didn't belong. I hung up on her in the middle of the tirade.